A Friday Barnes Mystery

GIRL DETECTIVE

ALSO BY R. A. SPRATT

*The Adventures of Nanny Piggins*
*Nanny Piggins and the Wicked Plan*
*Nanny Piggins and the Runaway Lion*

FRIDAY BARNES MYSTERIES

*Girl Detective*
*Under Suspicion*
*Big Trouble*

# A Friday Barnes Mystery

# GIRL DETECTIVE

### R. A. Spratt

*Illustrations by* **Phil Gosier**

SQUARE
FISH

Roaring Brook Press • New York

**SQUARE**
**FISH**

An imprint of Macmillan Publishing Group, LLC
175 Fifth Avenue
New York, NY 10010
mackids.com

GIRL DETECTIVE: A FRIDAY BARNES MYSTERY. Text copyright © 2014
by R. A. Spratt. Illustrations copyright © 2016 by Phil Gosier.
All rights reserved. Printed in the United States of America by LSC
Communications US, LLC (Lakeside Classic), Harrisonburg, Virginia

Square Fish and the Square Fish logo are trademarks of Macmillan and
are used by Roaring Brook Press under license from Macmillan.

Our books may be purchased in bulk for promotional, educational, or
business use. Please contact your local bookseller or the Macmillan
Corporate and Premium Sales Department at (800) 221-7945 ext. 5442
or by e-mail at MacmillanSpecialMarkets@macmillan.com.

Library of Congress Cataloging-in-Publication Data

Spratt, R. A.
    Friday Barnes, girl detective / by R. A. Spratt ; illustrations by Phil Gosier.
        pages cm
    "First published in Australia in 2014 by Penguin Random House Australia."
    Summary: "A genius girl detective discovers her ultra exclusive boarding
school is a hotbed of crime, from missing homework and stolen lemon tarts to
a mysterious yeti haunting the school swamp"—Provided by publisher.
    ISBN 978-1-250-14197-2 (paperback)    ISBN 978-1-250-14198-9 (ebook)
    [1. Boarding schools—Fiction.   2. Schools—Fiction.   3. Genius—Fiction.
4. Mystery and detective stories.]   I. Gosier, Phil, 1971–   illustrator.   II. Title.
PZ7.S76826Fri 2016
[Fic]—dc23

                                                          2015005923

First published in Australia in 2014 by Penguin Random House Australia
First published in the United States by Roaring Brook Press
First Square Fish Edition: 2017
Book designed by Anne Diebel
Square Fish logo designed by Filomena Tuosto

1  3  5  7  9  10  8  6  4  2

AR: 5.8

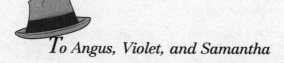

*To Angus, Violet, and Samantha*

# Chapter

# 1

# The Beginning

Friday Barnes was not an unhappy child. That said, she wasn't deliriously over the moon either. She was just left to get on with things. You see, Friday Barnes was the youngest of five children. Now, I know what you're thinking: "Five children! Her mother must have been so busy. What a workload! What a chaotic house they must have had!" Well, that's not how it was at all.

Friday's mother was a very systematic woman. You don't get a PhD in theoretical physics if you're not good at being methodical. And that is how Mrs. Barnes approached child rearing. She decided she wanted children, so she allocated four and a half years out of her career to have them. She spaced them exactly eighteen months apart, and when the oldest started school and the younger two were in day care, she went back to work.

Now, I'm sure if you're good at math, you will have noticed that if you have children eighteen months apart over a four-and-a-half-year period, that gives you four children in total. Mr. and Mrs. Barnes had their four children, and everything went according to plan. They taught them to read with flash cards, they sent them to the best after-school math courses, and they even allowed them to participate in sports. If you call yoga a sport.

Then, nine years later, just as their youngest child was gaining early admission to high school, the unexpected happened: Mrs. Barnes got pregnant again. There was no time in her schedule for childbirth. On the due date, she was committed to speak at a conference in Bern, Switzerland, about the possibility of the

International Super Collider opening a black hole and destroying the planet. For the first time in her adult life, Mrs. Barnes saw her ironclad grasp on order and reason begin to slip.

Mr. Barnes was, however, a man of action. That is, if the action did not require him to leave his office or get up from his desk. He Googled "Bern" and "maternity hospitals." They discovered that there was one just two miles from the conference center. Mr. and Mrs. Barnes both breathed a sigh of relief. From that moment on, life proceeded exactly as if Friday did not exist.

Late in her third trimester Mrs. Barnes traveled to Switzerland and gave her lecture. Halfway through she started to feel labor pains, but she was able to hold on till the end of her PowerPoint presentation. And only the people in the front row noticed when her water broke.

And so after a short taxi ride to the hospital and just seventeen hours in labor Friday was born. And she was named Friday because her parents thought that was the day of the week. (Being academics, they often became confused about such trivial matters as times and dates.) It was actually a Thursday.

Eleven years later, Friday Barnes had largely raised

herself. She was fairly small and dull-looking, with light brown hair and muddy brown eyes, and she had mastered the trick of finding the exact spot in a room with the least light, so that if she stood perfectly still nobody would notice she was there.

Even though she was only eleven, Friday was nearly ready to enter seventh grade because when she was five she had walked out on her first lesson in kindergarten (she didn't care for finger painting) and put herself straight into first grade. And this being Friday, none of the teachers noticed.

Friday found it was best to go unnoticed as much as possible. Being noticed just caused trouble. If her mother noticed Friday was eating an entire one-pound block of chocolate, she would take it away and tell her to eat an apple. If she didn't notice, Friday could eat as much as she liked.

Now, this may sound wonderful to many of you: to have uninterested parents who never interfere with anything you do. But the problem is that when you devote your entire time to going unnoticed by your parents, that talent seeps over into every other aspect of your life. Friday went unnoticed at school, on the bus, and at shops as well.

And if no one notices you, then no one talks to you, and if you spend your entire childhood in silence, you will not develop very good social skills. It is hard to make friends when your idea of a conversation starter is "How many moles of acid do you use to make your hair turn that shade of yellow?"

So at school, while all the other kids were playing, giggling, and gossiping, Friday would just read—a lot.

She had become so bored the summer she turned eight that she began reading every single book her parents had in the house. They had quite a few books (several thousand to be exact), many of which were on painfully dull subjects involving the minutiae of chemistry and physics. But Friday read quickly, so it only took her a year and a half to get through them all. As a result, Friday's schoolteachers rarely had any information to share with her that she did not already know, so they left her alone to sit at her desk at the back of the room reading detective novels.

Friday enjoyed these, because being a detective seemed to give a person license to behave very eccentrically indeed. Yet people were always so glad to see you. They were especially glad to see you when their mother-in-law had just been murdered and they were desperate to prove that, despite holding the blood-stained murder weapon, they were entirely innocent. But the best thing about detective novels was that if she concentrated really hard on solving the mystery, Friday was, for a little while, able to forget how lonely she was.

There was one adult Friday was particularly fond of: her uncle Bernie. He was an ex-cop who worked as an investigator for an insurance company. He baby-sat Friday every Thursday night. This was her favorite night of the week because as soon as her parents pulled out of the driveway, Uncle Bernie would throw out the macrobiotic lasagna her mother had left for their dinner, order two pizzas, and let Friday watch TV. Actual commercial TV, not just documentaries on PBS.

On this particular Thursday night, Uncle Bernie was clearly dis-tracted.

"Are you all right?" asked Friday. "You've been sighing very loudly, which leads me to deduce that either you have an upper respira-tory tract infection that is inhibiting your body's ability to absorb oxygen or something is troubling you."

"There is something," replied Uncle Bernie. "I'm under a lot of pressure at work from the CEO."

"He actually spoke to you?" asked Friday. "I thought he was always playing golf."

"He called from the ninth hole," said Uncle Bernie. "He was waiting for security to come and remove some lady golfers so he could play through, and he gave me a call."

"So what's his problem? Is it about your diabolical dress sense?" asked Friday with concern. "Have members of the public been making complaints?"

"What?" said Uncle Bernie.

"For a start, there is the fedora you insist on wearing," said Friday.

"It's traditional for great detectives to wear silly hats," said Uncle Bernie defensively.

"I suppose I can see how it would make a suspect underestimate you," said Friday.

"The problem is with a case," said Uncle Bernie. "I'm working on a bank robbery. A diamond worth five million dollars was stolen from a safe deposit box at the central branch of First National Bank."

"One diamond worth five million dollars?!" exclaimed Friday. "That's outrageous! Don't they know diamonds are just compressed carbon, and carbon is everywhere? In pencils, in wood, in every cell of our bodies?"

"Yes, but cells and pencils don't make sparkly jewelry," said Uncle Bernie. "I've got to catch who did it and get the diamond back, or our insurance company is out of pocket six million dollars."

"I thought you said it was worth five million dollars," said Friday.

"It is, but the policy has an additional one million for pain and suffering," explained Uncle Bernie. "The company really wants that diamond back. They're even offering a fifty-thousand-dollar reward to anyone who provides information that leads to its return."

"Fifty thousand dollars!" Friday exclaimed. Then, in the only athletic action she had taken in the last five years since she had run away from the doctor trying to give her a tetanus shot, she leaped over the couch. "Why didn't you say so? Let me see that paperwork."

# A Brilliant Deduction

Friday was onto her third lollipop and she still hadn't solved it. She had pored over the paperwork, surveillance videos, and affidavits from all the bank staff. The problem was that there was nothing to see. Everything in the bank vault proceeded according to protocol.

Friday watched the footage over and over again, focusing on all the details: the nervous way the bank manager kept touching his tie as he accompanied the appraiser

down to the vault; the way the appraiser methodically cleaned first one lens of his glasses and then the other before handling the stone; the number of times the security guard sneezed per minute, and the way Mr. Friedricks strode into the bank in his built-up cowboy boots, and towered over the average-height security guard as he

presented his card with a little flourish of the fingertips. Finally, there was the pandemonium as Mr. Friedricks discovered the diamond was missing and raised the alarm.

A siren went off. Staff ran down from the offices above, and in the chaos Mr. Friedricks must have stubbed his toe because he hobbled as he was ushered upstairs. Friday watched it all time and time again, trying to unravel the story of what really happened.

Suddenly Uncle Bernie, who had fallen asleep in front of the TV, woke up with a start.

"What time is it?" he asked.

"Quarter to twelve," said Friday.

"What?!" exclaimed Uncle Bernie as he leaped up from the couch. "We've got to hide the pizza boxes, de-tune the commercial channels, and put you in bed. Your parents could be here any second."

"It's all right. They won't be here for another fifteen minutes," said Friday, not looking up from the paperwork. "They are never early or late. They make complex calculations on traffic speed based on all the latest available data before they go anywhere in a car."

"Well, you should be in bed," said Uncle Bernie. "It's a school night."

"The most effective use of my time would be to sleep in school," said Friday. "Although I doubt I will be going to school tomorrow."

"Why?" asked Uncle Bernie.

"Because you are going to take me down to the bank so I can prove who committed this crime, discover where the diamond is hidden, and claim the fifty-thousand-dollar reward," announced Friday.

# 3

# The Bank Vault

It was eight in the morning and the bank hadn't opened yet. Uncle Bernie had, as per Friday's instructions, assembled the police chief, the bank manager, the security guard who had been on duty, the CEO of the insurance company, his secretary

(he never went anywhere without his secretary just in case he needed a cup of tea at a moment's notice), and the owner of the diamond, Mr. Friedricks, whose monstrous claim the insurance company desperately didn't want to pay out. Everyone had been instructed to dress in precisely the same clothes they were wearing the afternoon of the robbery.

"Can we move this along?" asked Mr. Friedricks as he checked his watch. "If this is going to be a complete waste of time I'd rather get it over with. I've got a trustees meeting at Highcrest Academy. It's the best school in the country and it took me two years to get on the board, so I don't want to be late for my first meeting."

"Is it a junior high or high school?" asked Friday.

"It's a combined school," said Mr. Friedricks. "What is this child doing here anyway?"

"Good question," agreed the police chief, taking out his notebook. "What's your name, young lady? I shall be passing it on to the social worker. Truancy is a crime, you know."

"Please, sir," said Uncle Bernie. "My niece may be eccentric, strange, small, dowdy, and inconsequential-looking—"

"I am?" asked Friday.

"But she's really very, very smart," continued Uncle Bernie. "She says she knows who did it, so she probably does."

"Then please get on with it," said the police chief.

"Let's review the evidence," declared Friday as she took Uncle Bernie's laptop and brought up the surveillance footage. "The bank was robbed last Tuesday. No one knows how the thief got in or got out. All we know is that when Mr. Friedricks came to withdraw the diamond at 2:17 p.m. on Tuesday afternoon, the diamond was no longer there. It had last been seen at 1 p.m. the previous day when an evaluator from the insurance company inspected the diamond for the official valuation."

"Yes, yes," said the police chief. "We all know the facts."

"You say that," said Friday, "but it's not true, because I know one fact more than any of you: the identity of the murderer!"

Friday was beginning to enjoy herself. She had been watching a lot of Agatha Christie movies, and she was beginning to speak with a trace of a Belgian accent and to twirl an imaginary mustache as she strutted about the vault like Hercule Poirot.

"Identity of the thief," corrected Uncle Bernie.

"Yes, yes, same difference," said Friday. "The video evidence from all the security cameras has been scoured. No one came into contact with the security box in that time, which means only one of three things can have happened. Number one, the security camera footage was tampered with."

"But the recordings for the security camera are housed in a titanium box," protested the bank manager, "and it's isolated from the Internet, so there is no way it could be broken into physically or by hacking into it."

"Exactly," agreed Friday. "The second alternative is that the thief used laparoscopic technology to drill a hole up through the subfloor and extract the diamond by tube."

"If that had occurred," said the police chief, "there would be filings and a one-inch-diameter hole big enough for the diamond to pass through."

"I know," agreed Friday, opening the security box to show the others. "And as you can see, there is no such hole."

"What's the third option?" asked the police chief. Like most lawmen, he loved a good crime mystery.

"That someone walked into the bank, went down to the safe deposit boxes, opened the box, and took it," said Friday.

"But you've just said that was impossible because no one was caught on film," said the bank manager.

"Ah, but he was caught on film," said Friday. "Only one person opened the box. And that person was . . . *Mr. Friedricks*!"

Friday pointed at Mr. Friedricks for dramatic effect. "When he opened the box he didn't discover the diamond was gone. He stole it."

Uncle Bernie groaned. "Oh dear, I'm going to lose my job over this."

"Why on earth would I steal my own diamond?" asked Mr. Friedricks.

"For the insurance money, of course," said Friday.

"This is an insult," said Mr. Friedricks. "I want this girl arrested for slander."

"You can't be arrested for slander, because it isn't a felony. You'd have to take civil action," explained the police chief. "Though I think you'd have a pretty good case. You've got plenty of reputable witnesses."

"But I can prove that I'm right," said Friday. "Take a look at this part of the security footage." Friday showed the point at which Mr. Friedricks arrived in the vault.

"But he's just entered," said the police chief. "He hasn't done anything yet."

"Look at this," said Friday as she slowly moved the footage forward frame by frame. "He is handing the security guard—"

"That's me," said the security guard proudly, pleased to see how slim he looked on screen.

"How's your cold?" asked Friday.

"How did you know I had a cold?" asked the security guard.

"Because you sneezed sixteen times in seven minutes while Mr. Friedricks was in the vault," said Friday. "You can't have hay fever, because you work in an airtight underground bank vault where there's no pollen, and you can't have the flu or you wouldn't be able to perform a job that required so much standing; therefore, I deduced a simple cold."

"I'm fine now, thank you," said the security guard.

"Can we get on with this?" asked the police chief.

"Yes, of course," said Friday, returning her attention to the surveillance footage on her computer screen.

"Here it is. Mr. Friedricks presenting his business card."

"So?" said Mr. Friedricks.

"Look at the flourish," said Friday. "He doesn't just hand over the card—he flicks it up into his fingertips. Normal people don't do that. The only people who use that little dramatic gesture to present a card are magicians."

"What?!" exclaimed the police chief.

"It takes hours and hours of practice to balance the card perfectly on your fingers to do that," said Friday. She took out one of her uncle's business cards and handed it to the police chief. "You try."

The police chief flicked the card up, but it slipped out of his fingers and fluttered to the ground.

"It's not easy," said Friday, "but Mr. Friedricks did it without even thinking. It was instinctual, automatic; it shows he has at some stage in his life spent years cultivating the techniques of sleight-of-hand magic."

"Preposterous," said Mr. Friedricks.

"And I was easily able to prove it was true," continued Friday, "because the Barnum and Bailey Circus Skills University does not have very good online security." Friday clicked away busily at the computer for a few moments. "So when I hacked into their transcript database I found that you, Mr. Friedricks, graduated magna cum laude twenty years ago with a major in acrobatics and a minor in sleight-of-hand." Friday turned the laptop around and showed everyone Mr. Friedricks's transcript.

"That doesn't prove anything," blustered Mr. Friedricks. "A man is entitled to have a misspent youth and start again without it being held against him."

"What are you saying, Friday?" asked Uncle Bernie.

"I'm saying that Mr. Friedricks had all the sleight-of-hand skills necessary to palm the diamond when he opened the box and pretended that it wasn't there," accused Friday.

"Hold on," said the bank manager. "When a theft is reported we have strict protocols. No one can leave the bank without being searched. Mr. Friedricks did not have the diamond on him when he left the bank."

"No," agreed Friday. "He had it under him."

"Does she always talk in riddles?" complained the CEO.

"Sometimes she can go days without talking at all," said Uncle Bernie.

"I wish this was one of those days," muttered the CEO.

"I draw your attention to Mr. Friedricks's boots," said Friday.

"Now it's a crime to wear boots, is it?" asked Mr. Friedricks.

"We'll see," said Friday. "You'll notice Mr. Friedricks is wearing boots with a three-inch Cuban heel."

"So?" asked the police sergeant.

"Why would a man who is six foot four—" began Friday.

"Six foot five," Mr. Friedricks interrupted.

Friday looked him up and down. "I think you'll find you have shrunk since you last measured your height." Friday turned back to the others. "Anyway, why would such a tall man deliberately choose a shoe with a three-inch heel? He already towers over most men. A shoe with a heel is much less comfortable, as any woman wearing heels can tell you."

The secretary nodded. She was wearing five-inch stilettos and they were killing her.

"Therefore," continued Friday, "the only possible reason Mr. Friedricks could have for wearing such ostentatious height-elevating shoes is so that they would have heels large enough for him to hollow one out and hide a diamond inside!"

Everyone looked at Mr. Friedricks's feet.

"This is an insult!" Mr. Friedricks exclaimed again. "Footwear is not probable cause."

"Not in and of itself," agreed Friday. "But when footwear is combined with a limp!"

Friday turned on the

surveillance footage again and Mr. Friedricks could be seen clutching his foot for a moment, then leaving the bank with a slight limp.

"A limp that you had when you left but not when you entered," added Friday. "That is incriminating evidence indeed."

"I'm not staying for this ridiculous child's fantasy. I've got a meeting to attend. Some hysterical student told a tabloid they saw a giant ape in the school swamp, and the board has to decide whether they want to sue the student for defamation," said Mr. Friedricks as he strode to the door. "If you've got anything further to say to me, you can say it to my lawyer."

"Show us your shoe first," said the police chief.

"Where's your search warrant?" demanded Mr. Friedricks.

"I don't need a warrant to search the shoe of a suspect in a bank robbery," said the police chief. "Now take off your shoe. I may look like an aging man to you, but I should inform you that back in my day I was the all-state wrestling champion for the police force three years in a row. And I had to wrestle against firefighters and paramedics, and they are tricky rascals who cheat."

Mr. Friedricks slowly and reluctantly bent down, slid off his boot, and showed it to the police chief. "There, you see? Nothing inside."

"Let me have a closer look," said the police chief. He inspected the boot very carefully. He took out the insole and looked over every stitch in the sole.

"Try twisting the heel," suggested Friday.

"That's an eight-hundred-dollar boot!" exclaimed the secretary, who had a great deal of respect for footwear, expensive footwear in particular.

The police chief held the shoe firmly and twisted on the heel. It pivoted on one of the boot nails, revealing a cavity within—a cavity that was the exact size and shape of a five-million-dollar diamond.

"Wow!" exclaimed Friday. "I was right. How exciting! I've only ever solved fictional crimes before."

"Why would that make him limp?" asked Uncle Bernie.

"If you had something worth five million dollars in your shoe wouldn't you walk funny?" asked Friday.

"But where is the diamond?" asked the police chief.

"You should search his office," suggested Friday. "He wouldn't hide it at home in case his maid or, worse, his wife found it. No, Mr. Friedricks would have more privacy in his workspace. It won't be in his desk or filing cabinets because there would be a danger that his secretary might stumble across it while looking for something else. So try the light fittings. Most corporate offices have ceilings that are only eight and a half feet high; therefore, Mr. Friedricks would be able to reach that easily without even standing on a chair."

"You've been spying on me, haven't you!" accused Mr. Friedricks (which inadvertently was a confession).

"No," said Friday, confused by the suggestion. "There was no need. All the information was right in front of me."

Mr. Friedricks was now making frantic but futile attempts to get out through the vault door. The police chief took great delight in dusting off some of his wrestling moves. He put Mr. Friedricks in a cobra lock, then handcuffed him.

"Thank you, young lady," said the police chief. "We were up on violent crime arrests this month, but down on white-collar criminals, so this is going to do wonders for our statistics."

The police chief led Mr. Friedricks away.

"I'm going to get you!" yelled Mr. Friedricks as he

was half dragged up the stairs by the police chief and security guard. "You won't get away with this! I'm a powerful man! You will regret crossing me."

"Please keep your voice down, sir," said the police chief. "Threatening a child will only add more years to your sentence."

"You're kidding yourself. I'm going to get the best lawyers in the country," said Mr. Friedricks. "I'll be out in no time with good behavior—then you just watch out."

"I'd steer clear of Friday in the future if I were you, Mr. Friedricks," Uncle Bernie called after him. "I think you've met your match in her."

Mr. Friedricks disappeared into the upstairs office area, his loud abuse fading into the distance.

"Call the golf course," the CEO snapped to his secretary. "See if you can get me a nine-fifteen tee-off. Barnes, I'll get accounts to cut a check for your niece here."

The CEO walked over to Friday and shook her hand. "Thank you, young lady. You have just saved my company a lot of money. And I haven't entirely lost my morning of golf. Fine work. Maybe we'll consult you again next time the professionals are out of their depth." The CEO glared at Uncle Bernie as he said this.

Uncle Bernie realized he had been insulted, but he didn't care. He wasn't going to be fired, at least not today, which was a big relief.

"Wow!" said Uncle Bernie. "Fifty thousand dollars is a lot of money. What are you going to do with it all?"

"I have an idea," said Friday.

# How Friday Spent the $50,000

Friday's parents were shocked to learn she had been awarded such a huge amount of money. They had never had anything like that large a sum in their own bank accounts. They were even more shocked when they learned how she intended to spend it.

"I'm sending myself to Highcrest Academy as a full-time boarding student for one year," announced Friday.

"I've recently heard it is the finest school in the country."

"You're moving out?" asked her bewildered mother.

"Yes," said Friday.

"But you're only nine," protested her equally bewildered father.

"I turned eleven last October," Friday pointed out. "You remember. You lent me your credit card so I could buy myself a mass spectrometer."

"Oh, I do remember," said her father. "I thought it odd because we had a perfectly good mass spectrometer in the garage."

"Yes, well, actually, I didn't buy a mass spectrometer," revealed Friday. "I bought an electric conversion kit for my bicycle because you keep forgetting to pick me up from school events, and I needed a way to get from A to B."

"Friday, you're getting off the point," Uncle Bernie reminded her. He was present to help explain things to her parents. Like many super-bright academic people who spend all day thinking about complicated tricky things, they could get totally flummoxed by the simplest everyday conversation.

"I've got fifty thousand dollars. What could be more

worthwhile than spending it on my education? So I've decided to send myself to the best and most expensive boarding school in the whole country," said Friday. "Besides, if I must attend school, then I'd like to go somewhere that operates on a profit motive."

"But why?" asked her father. Capitalism baffled him. It all seemed like such a lot of effort.

"Because I want to do something different," said Friday.

Her parents still looked at her blankly.

"Quantum, Quasar, Orion, and Halley all went to the same schools." (These were the names of Friday's brothers and sisters.) "Now all six of you are university academics researching theoretical physics. I want to do something else."

"So study particle physics," suggested her father.

"Or astrophysics," suggested her mother.

"Also, because if they operate on a profit motive," said Friday, ignoring their response, "the PE teachers will accept bribes, so that I am never forced to run cross-country again."

Friday's parents considered this. It was a concept that made sense to them.

"Hmm," said Friday's father. He put the end of his

pen between his teeth and started chewing on it. He didn't suck on lollipops but he had his own habit for when he was lost in deep thought. And this was quite a conundrum for him. He was going to have to buy another twelve-pack of Bic pens. It was clearly a multi-pen problem.

"Why don't you reflect on the issue?" suggested Friday. "Then you could write me a paper outlining the pros and cons of my decision."

"That's a good idea," said Friday's mother, brightening up. She liked writing papers.

"I'll give you two months to write it," said Friday. "You need to consider the issues thoroughly."

"I don't know," said Friday's father, looking concerned.

"Would you prefer three months?" guessed Friday.

"I think you had better make it four," said Friday's father. "We may need to do research."

"With a control group," said Friday's mother.

"Obviously," agreed Friday's father.

And that's how Friday knew she had won. Because the starting date at her new school was in seven weeks. By the time her parents had finished their paper; handed it in three weeks late (it is traditional in academic spheres to hand in all papers at least three weeks late); waited four weeks for her response (which she had no intention of giving); then forgotten the day of the week, month, and year and moved on with their research, she would be well into her second semester at her new school and it would be churlish of them to try to withdraw her at that point.

# Chapter
# 5
# A New Chapter

It had not occurred to Friday to be nervous about starting a new school. School was something she was good at. Normal concerns about whether she would make any friends did not occur to Friday because she had never made any friends, unless you counted long-dead authors like Jane Austen, Charles Dickens, and Charlotte Brontë (and her former school psychologist did not).

When Friday packed her suitcase to leave for her new school, her only concern was whether she would fit all her favorite books in her suitcase, not what clothes she would look good in to make a first impression. The first impression she wanted to make was no impression. She wanted to go unnoticed.

Friday had long ago found that a certain shade of brown cardigan when paired with jeans was even more effective than complete military-grade camouflage if you wanted to blend into any situation and go unnoticed. Khaki is great in your average jungle, but if you dress head to toe in khaki and then try to borrow a book from the local library, everyone will stare. Whereas if you wear a brown cardigan, you can hide both in the library and in the bushes outside the library—whichever you prefer to do.

There was the matter of how Friday was going to get to the school. Uncle Bernie had offered to give Friday a lift, but then his car broke down. While Friday was an excellent self-taught mechanic with an extensive working knowledge of the internal combustion engine, she didn't have access to a foundry or molten iron, so there was not much she could do about the crack in his head gasket. Uncle Bernie felt terrible about it. He took a taxi over to Friday's house to give her a special parting gift.

"You didn't have to get me anything," said Friday. "I already have a full supply of pens and pencils."

"Friday, I didn't get you something because I thought you needed something," explained Uncle Bernie. "I got you something because I'm going to miss you."

"Oh," said Friday. She suddenly found she had a lump in her throat. She knew it was unlikely to be a growth. This lump was the symptom of emotions, one of the few things she knew very little about. "Don't worry, I'm sure you'll find someone else to watch TV with on Thursday nights. You could disable one of your neighbors' cable TV boxes, then invite them over to watch with you."

"I'm going to miss you," said Uncle Bernie. "And I'm going to worry about you being up at that school all on your own."

"I've always been all on my own," said Friday.

"I know," agreed Uncle Bernie. "But you've been on your own in the comfort of your home. Trust me, living with a couple hundred rich kids is going to be different. If you have any problems, I want you to let me know. I want you to stay in touch. That's why I'm giving you a present. Open it."

Friday opened the package. "A portable ham radio?" she said. She was surprised and delighted.

"I read the Highcrest Academy school rules from cover to cover," explained Uncle Bernie. "They list all banned electronic devices: computers, smartphones, MP3 players, tablets, video games, Wi-Fi–capable calculators, and laser pointers. But they didn't say anything about ham radios."

"Thanks, Uncle Bernie, for everything. I'm going to miss you, too," said Friday, giving him an awkward hug. "This is the nicest gift anyone has given me since Aunt Gerta sent me the noise-canceling headphones."

So on the first Monday of her first term, Friday found herself having to travel to her new school by bus. Generally, she did not care for buses because she was so good at going unnoticed that people would often sit on her, thinking she was an empty seat.

When she arrived at Highcrest Academy, Friday looked as though she had spent seven hours squashed, as indeed she had. The bus dropped her on the street outside the school, which unfortunately meant she was still nearly a mile from the nearest school building because the campus had such an unnecessarily long driveway (either to intimidate those arriving at the school, or to intimidate unathletic children who were considering running away).

Friday started walking slowly up the driveway as a constant stream of expensive imported cars and excessively safe SUVs drove by, kicking up dust and gravel as they passed. Friday's feet, or perhaps it was her heart, seemed to grow heavier with each step toward the neo-Gothic buildings. She tried to take her mind off her growing sense of foreboding by mentally translating the lyrics of the national anthem into Morse code.

When Friday finally arrived at the main building she saw a busy scene. The high school students had

arrived two days earlier and were buzzing about the school as they moved between their classes. But all the junior high students were arriving that day, so a lot of children were being dropped off by parents, nannies, and chauffeurs. Friday had to wind her way around them, carrying her backpack and dragging a heavy suitcase.

Friday may not have been a self-conscious girl, but she was observant. So as she made her way through the crowd she began to notice the other children. They were very well dressed, immaculately dressed in fact. And their clothes were not only ironed (a condition in which no item of clothing could ever be found in the Barnes household) but also expensive brands. The children were dressed head to toe in designer clothing. At Friday's old school, one such item of daywear would be enough to mark you well-to-do and lead to your lunch being stolen by someone hungry for gourmet food.

Friday began to realize she may have made a tactical error. Her brown cardigan was not going to blend in here. And all she had to wear were three pairs of jeans, seven gray T-shirts, and three brown cardigans. There was no school uniform to save her. Or, rather, there was a school uniform, but it was an unofficial one that all the rich children intuitively knew about, whereas Friday, for whom fashion intuition was one of her few weaknesses, had not received a copy of the unwritten message. Friday started to feel hot, her breathing accelerated, her chest tight—she recognized these symptoms from her first day at preschool. (This was before she had discovered her brown cardigan uniform and she'd made the mistake of wearing a lab coat and rubber gloves because she had heard that four-year-olds were unhygienic.) She was having a fashion-related anxiety attack. Hopefully she would be able to hide in her dorm room before anyone noticed her.

But that was not to be. When she reached the top of the driveway, Friday looked up to take in Highcrest Academy. The two-story stone building had broad columns, making it look more like a museum or a courthouse than a school. Behind the main building Friday could see a long redbrick dormitory. And beyond that were rolling lawns, which surrounded the buildings on all four sides. The grass was so perfectly manicured it looked like a golf course at a Masters tournament. Friday was sure if she tried to set foot on it, an irate greenkeeper would leap out of a bush and insist she take her shoes off. Even the banisters leading up the front steps into the school were made of brass and had been so highly polished Friday could see her own scared face in them. She was not an athletically inclined girl, but at that moment she felt a welling urge to turn and run.

Then chaos erupted.

"Aaaagggghhhh!!!" There was a blood-curdling scream from behind her.

Friday was almost relieved to hear someone other than herself scream. Evidently, she was not the only one overwhelmed to be starting a new school.

She turned to see an older boy stumble out of the bushes. His face was white and his eyes were wide with shock. "I just . . . saw it," panted the boy, struggling to catch his breath. "Down by the swamp. It was half man, half beast. It was horrible."

Friday was so astonished by this unexpectedly dramatic announcement that she instinctively took a step back, which was a mistake. If she had been looking she would have seen the Lexus SUV approaching. She couldn't hear it because the image-conscious driver had bought the hybrid model with an almost silent electric engine. So it came as a complete surprise to Friday when she heard screeching rubber and slipping brakes, and looked to see the SUV right before it slammed into her suitcase, which slammed into her, causing her to stumble and bang her head on an ornamental statue of Socrates.

Friday kept her eyes tightly closed. In the past she had found that if she kept her eyes closed, pain and blood didn't seem so bad. It was opening your eyes and taking it all in that made the situation overwhelming. She mentally recited the digits of pi to distract herself. She didn't want the entire student body's first impression of her to be lying on the ground crying.

"Sorry, didn't see you there," said a man's voice. Obviously, the brown cardigan was still working, but a little

bit too well. "I'll be there on Thursday. Don't let anyone do anything until I arrive."

Friday thought this was a slightly odd statement.
She had just hit her head on a sandstone representa-
tion of an ancient Greek philosopher. Clearly she
needed medical attention. Waiting until Thursday
would be irresponsible. Then she realized the man was
not talking to her; he was talking on his phone, which
would also explain how he had come to hit an enormous suitcase in the driveway of the school.

"Mr. Peterson, there is a five-mile-per-hour speed
limit within the school grounds," chided a woman as
she rushed forward to help Friday. "You've hit a student!"

"Technically, he hit a suitcase, which hit a girl, who
fell over and hit a statue," said an airy girl's voice.

"Yes, thank you, Melanie, that's quite enough," said
the nice woman.

Mr. Peterson put his hand over the mouthpiece of
the phone. "Send me the bill for the medical expenses,
and if she wants to sue, put her in touch with my
lawyer," he said before taking his hand away from the
mouthpiece and resuming his other conversation.
"Sorry about that. Some girl just put her suitcase in

front of my car. No, no, everything's fine. It's just a rental car."

Friday opened her eyes. Everything was fuzzy at first. But then things began to swim into focus. There seemed to be hundreds of faces staring down at her. The faces mainly belonged to children, many of whom were sniggering. But there was one adult face in the middle. She was a pretty young woman who looked concerned. "Are you hurt?" the nice lady asked.

Friday considered this. "I don't think so," she said. "I think my suitcase took the brunt of it." (It was a good thing she had packed so many books.)

"Your head is bleeding," said the nice lady.

"It is?" asked Friday. She touched her forehead, and when she drew her hand away it was covered in cherry-red blood. "Oh dear, I don't like blood." Which was an understatement, because Friday promptly fainted.

# The Nice Lady

Friday awoke sometime later in a lovely sunny room that was full of birds. At least it seemed that way at first. As Friday's senses returned she was able to distinguish that she was in a beautifully tidy classroom with high bench tables and stools. More spectacularly, all along one wall was an enormous aviary full of the most colorful and exotic birds.

"Am I dead?" asked Friday optimistically. She hoped heaven would be somewhere this lovely.

"No," said the nice lady, who was still beside her. "You're in the biology classroom."

"It's wonderful," approved Friday. "Are you a nurse?"

"Goodness no," said the nice lady. "I'm Miss Harrow, the biology teacher."

"Oh, I'm terribly sorry," said Friday.

"Why do you say that?" asked Miss Harrow.

"Well, there is no way someone as nice as you could become a biology teacher without there having been some dreadful life event that forced you to deviate from a preferable path," said Friday. "If you were clever at biology you'd be much better off being a research scientist, a pharmacologist, or an evil-genius inventor living under a volcano and thinking up clever ways to take over the world. Or better yet, you could marry someone who was a research scientist, a pharmacologist, or an evil-genius inventor and then you could stay home all day reading novels."

"That isn't the case," said Miss Harrow. "I'm just good at biology and I like working with children."

"But no one likes working with children," argued Friday. "They're unhygienic and disrespectful, and they have a limited resource of information on which to draw their small talk."

"*You're* a child," Miss Harrow pointed out.

"Which is how I know," said Friday. "I spend all day surrounded by them."

"Anyway, one of the parents is a plastic surgeon," continued Miss Harrow, "so he put eight stitches in your forehead and diagnosed you with a mild concussion."

"I was treated by a plastic surgeon for a bump on the head?" asked Friday.

"The school will just add the bill to Mr. Peterson's account," Miss Harrow assured her, "so don't worry about that."

"Oh, I wasn't planning on starting my first day by initiating legal proceedings," said Friday. "I like to go unnoticed, and serving people with court summonses can really irritate them. I know—I learned that the hard way when I sued my kindergarten teacher for sending me to the naughty corner."

"Why did she send you to the naughty corner?" asked Miss Harrow curiously.

"For refusing to participate in finger painting," said Friday. "I argued that one of the primary features that distinguishes man from animals is that we are able to use tools; therefore, to finger-paint is devolutionary."

"I can see how that would rub a kindergarten teacher the wrong way," said Miss Harrow sympathetically. "How's your head?"

Friday tentatively dabbed her forehead and found that it did not hurt. In fact she couldn't feel it at all.

She hoped this was due to a local anesthetic and not to unilateral nerve damage. "It seems fine," she said.

"Well, if you're feeling up to it, you'd better get along to your room. Otherwise your roommate will have hogged all the drawer space and hidden your things in a bush down by the swamp."

"Is that sort of thing common?" asked Friday.

"Tremendously so," said Miss Harrow. "The school has to keep two gardeners on duty first day back, purely for retrieving property from boggy bushes. You see, most of the students here aren't used to having to squeeze their possessions into just twelve square yards of floor space with one built-in wardrobe and a bookcase. That's why students are always so keen to get here as soon as the gates open. The bedroom turf war is a bitter, cruelty-ridden saga that will never end, not without some sort of UN intervention."

Friday was beginning to worry about her books. It was one thing to throw someone's clothing into a swamp—clothes could be washed—but books were another matter. Mud and books did not mix well. Or, rather, they mixed too well and formed impenetrable bonds, involving pages swelling, ink running, and covers hardening.

"I'd better be off," said Friday, sliding off the chair.

She then slid onto the floor, because apparently all the blood she had lost in the accident had been from her head. But she found the cool linoleum pressed against her face reviving and so, with the aid of the kind Miss Harrow, she was on her feet again, this time more slowly. Friday made it to the door, only tripping once on a loose panel in the floor when a voice bellowed out from above. "Friday Barnes, please report to the Headmaster's office."

Friday was still fairly brain-addled from her head injury. "Did you hear that," she asked Miss Harrow, "or has a bruise in my brain tissue caused me to start having auditory hallucinations?"

"No, you heard it," said Miss Harrow reassuringly. "It's just the school's public address system. There are speakers in every room. You'd better hurry along to the Headmaster's office. He doesn't approve of tardiness. Not in others anyway."

"I'm not going to get in trouble for banging my head, am I?" worried Friday. She was pretty sure she was the victim in this situation.

"Oh no, of course not," said Miss Harrow. "At least I don't think so."

# 8

# The Headmaster's Office

When she arrived at the Headmaster's office Friday found she had company. There was already another girl sitting on the hard wooden bench outside. Friday dropped her backpack and slumped down at the far end of the long seat. She was in no mood to make chit-chat. Her brain had data to analyze. Unfortunately, the other girl on the bench did not appreciate the necessity of silence to Friday's thought process. She sobbed loudly.

Friday looked across at her. The girl was pretty, blond, and— what is the polite way to put

this?—not fat but not thin either. She looked like the type of girl who spent very little time being unhappy. Normally, the sun would shine on her and she would good-naturedly shine back. But something had clearly upset her now. The girl's pouting lower lip quivered, and her eyes brimmed with tears. Friday judged that if she did not say precisely the right thing, this girl would soon be sobbing on her shoulder.

It is widely considered that the best thing to say to an upset person is something reassuring, but actually, if you don't want to be cried on, the opposite is true. Young girls in trouble are desperately keen to have a good cry. They will seize the first opportunity to grab hold of someone and cry all over them. So Friday had the good sense to try the opposite tactic.

"Man up!" ordered Friday. "There will be no crying here today. Do you understand me?"

The girl's lip quivered more. But then she gave a hearty sniff and seemed to compose herself just a fraction. "Okay," she said, with only the tiniest of sobs.

"I've had a difficult day, so I'd appreciate it if you didn't—" began Friday, but she never got to complete her sentence. The other girl scooched across the length of the bench, grabbed Friday's forearm, and looked pleadingly into her eyes.

"I didn't do it," blubbered the girl. There were definitely teary sobs starting to leak out now. "I've been wrongly accused."

And that did it. Friday was suddenly able to set her own concerns to the back burner of her mind as she focused on the irresistible challenge this girl had just blubbed to her.

"Wrongly accused of what?" asked Friday as she scooched closer herself.

"Stealing the Albert Singh Memorial Carriage Clock from the Headmaster's desk," said the girl, at which point she burst into tears, having found Friday to be sufficiently sympathetic to cry all over.

Friday patted the girl on the shoulder as her eyes leaked and her shoulders heaved. This girl was obviously an expert crier. No doubt she had acquired all sorts of ponies and laptop computers by using just this technique on her own father. The most touching thing about her sniffly blubbering was that it was clearly sincere.

Friday came to her first conclusion. Either this girl was a brilliant actress, which was unlikely because a brilliant actress would tone it back a bit, or she did not have the meanness of spirit, imagination, or guile requisite to commit such a symbolic crime.

"Please, please, you must help me," begged the girl.

"Why do you think I would be able to do that?" asked Friday in surprise. Her being awarded $50,000 for solving the bank robbery had not been publicized. There was no earthly reason why this girl would know she was secretly a master criminologist.

"I'll give you anything," said the girl, sitting back so that she could look pleadingly into Friday's eyes.

"Like what?" asked Friday, her curiosity again piqued.

"Jewelry?" suggested the girl.

"I haven't got time for that sort of trumpery," said Friday dismissively.

"Clothes," suggested the girl, eyeing Friday's discount-store red sneakers.

Here she had touched a nerve. Friday looked at the beautiful girl sitting next to her. It wasn't just that she was better-looking. It was almost as if the girl was an alien life form from another planet. Her physical appearance was so much more aesthetically appealing than her own. "I don't think your clothes would fit me," said Friday. This girl was at least six inches taller and thirty pounds heavier.

"How about money?" suggested the girl. "I've got lots of that. I've got a trust fund, plus an allowance, plus a lovely old aunt who writes to me and tucks fifty dollars in the envelope, then forgets about it because she's senile and writes to me again. Sometimes she writes to me three times a day."

This sparked Friday's interest. She realized spending $50,000 to get into the country's most elite boarding school was all very good, but she would need funds to get by while she was there. "I do like money," admitted Friday. "How much have you got?"

"Lots and lots," said the girl, starting to cheer up.

"I'll do it," said Friday. "I'll prove your innocence for the fee of five hundred dollars."

The girl laughed. "That will be no problem. I've got that much tucked in my sock right now."

"Oh," said Friday. "I think I'd prefer it if my payment was made in money that had not spent time in your footwear." A girl who knew as much about bacteria as she did was ever mindful of hygiene.

"Of course, of course," said the girl. "Whatever you like. But you have to do it quickly, because the Headmaster has just called my father. He will be here first thing tomorrow morning to pick me up. You have to prove my innocence before then. Daddy doesn't like it when I'm expelled."

"Do you get expelled often?" asked Friday.

"Oh yes," confessed the girl. "I got expelled from my last school for hitchhiking into town to buy chocolate. I would have gotten away with it, too, if the driver who picked me up hadn't been a kidnapper who decided to hold me for ransom."

"I remember that case," said Friday, impressed to

be sitting next to a celebrity in the world of crime, or more precisely, a victim of crime. "I read about it in the papers. You must be Delia Michaels."

"That's right," said Delia, happy to be recognized.

"And you were rescued because your captor accidentally ate a peanut and went into anaphylactic shock, so you had to call an ambulance and perform CPR on her until the paramedics arrived," recalled Friday.

"Yes, that's me," agreed Delia. "I got a bravery medal for it."

"Hmm," said Friday, privately concluding that Delia should have been given a silliness medal instead. "So what exactly have you been accused of this time?"

"Stealing the clock that was presented to the school by Albert Singh," explained Delia. "He was the first person to climb Mount Everest with the aid of suction shoes."

"And why are you the chief suspect?" asked Friday.

"Last night I was caught sneaking out of the Headmaster's office after lights-out," answered Delia.

"What happened?" asked Friday. "Did someone drug you and leave you in there to frame you for the crime?"

"Oh no," said Delia truthfully. "I broke in. I climbed through the window above the door."

Friday looked up to see a small ventilation window directly above the door to the Headmaster's office. "That must have taken significant agility and upper-body strength," said Friday.

"Not really," admitted Delia. "I borrowed a little stepladder from the janitor's closet. The hard part was falling down on the other side. I should have brought a pillow to land on."

"I'm impressed," said Friday. She had not imagined that Delia had it in her to actually plan a crime. "But it all sounds very incriminating."

"I know," wailed Delia. "What am I going to do?"

"Leave it to me," said Friday reassuringly. She couldn't help but like this disarmingly attractive and weepy girl. "I'll break into the office and find the evidence to prove your innocence."

"But then you'll get expelled, too," wailed Delia even louder.

"I doubt it," said Friday. "As long as I'm right, which I usually am, the Headmaster would be very churlish to expel me for a little harmless breaking and entering. Come along." Friday got up and went over to examine the lock on the Headmaster's door.

"You want to do it now?!" exclaimed Delia. "In broad daylight?"

"It's always better to perpetrate crimes in broad daylight," said Friday as she riffled through her backpack before taking a tension wrench, a stethoscope, and a homemade lock pick made from a flattened piece of umbrella hinge. "You bump into fewer things if you can see what you're doing. And people get tremendously grumpy if they have to get out of bed in the middle of the night to confront you with your misdeeds." Friday knelt on the floor, put the stethoscope in her ears and the other end against the lock, inserted the pick and tension wrench into the shaft, and started jiggling the pins with her pick.

"How long is this going to take?" asked Delia, nervously looking about. "Someone could walk by at any moment."

"Picking a lock usually takes between seven and fifteen minutes," said Friday as she concentrated on her task. "It is not a matter of skill, as commonly depicted. It is a matter of trial and error and the inherent luck in dealing with any matter that involves the law of probability."

The lock clicked open.

"Fortunately for us, our Headmaster has chosen a very cheap lock," said Friday with a smile.

It was a large, elegant room that had been ostentatiously decorated with antiques and leather-bound books, to remind whoever sat down in front of the desk that the man on the other side was extremely important.

Delia didn't want to be spotted by a passerby in the corridor, so she moved to step into the room.

Friday stopped her. "Stay still," whispered Friday. "This is a crime scene. You must not touch anything, especially with your feet."

From her position in the doorway Friday systematically scanned every detail in the room. "Lend me your phone," she said to Delia.

"I don't have one," said Delia. "It's against school rules."

"I know you have a phone in your inside jacket pocket," said Friday, "because it dug into my shoulder when you collapsed on me weeping. I'm sure that someone with the means to bribe a member of the janitorial staff can get a phone smuggled into a boarding school."

Delia reluctantly took the phone from her jacket and handed it to Friday. But Friday didn't make any calls. Instead she turned on the camera function and started taking close-up pictures of the carpet. She systematically crawled over every inch of the floor, taking photos of everything.

"Can you hurry up?" whispered Delia urgently. "The Headmaster is sure to return soon."

"I don't know what you're worried about," said Friday as she moved on to the desk and started taking even closer photographs of seemingly nothing, because the desk was entirely empty. "You're being expelled anyway. It's not like things can get any worse for you."

"You don't know my father," said Delia sadly. "He's been sending away for brochures to military school."

"Your father is not going to send you to military school," said Friday, who now produced a tape measure and notebook, and started jotting down precise notes about all the measurements of the desk.

"He's not?" asked the girl.

"No, you are habitually clumsy," said Friday. "The scuff marks on your shoes show that you trip an unusual amount. You are flighty and emotional. Any sensible man would not want a child like that to be trained in the use of firearms, and I presume your father must be a sensible man, because he can afford to send you here. No, if he's really cross with you, the worst he'll do is send you to a public school."

Delia gasped. "Noooo!" she cried.

"Shhh," said Friday. "Someone will hear you."

And Friday was entirely right because the next second the Headmaster burst into the office.

"What is the meaning of this?!"

# A Problem Solved

Ah, Headmaster," said Friday. "My name is Friday Barnes. Pleased to meet you." She held out her hand for him to shake, but he ignored it. "My acquaintance Delia Michaels has asked me to investigate the wrongful allegation against her regarding the theft of the memorial carriage clock on your desk."

"Of all the impertinence—" began the Headmaster.

"Before you continue,"

interrupted Friday, "you should know I can prove she did not take it. So if I were you, I'd hear me out before you made any wild allegations, which Delia's no doubt litigious father would not be happy to hear about."

The Headmaster visibly warred with himself. His eye twitched as he pressed his lips together and scowled. He was in his early sixties and had been a teacher for over forty years, so he could remember the days when you were allowed to whack children for being naughty— and he missed those days dreadfully. "She was caught red-handed, sneaking out of my office with my spare keys in her hand," seethed the Headmaster, struggling to maintain his indoor voice.

"You didn't tell me that," said Friday, turning to Delia. "That is pretty incriminating."

"I know," sobbed Delia. "I guess going to military school won't be so bad. I'm not afraid of marching. It's the haircut I'm worried about."

"Never fear," said Friday. "Your golden locks are safe. Because I can prove it wasn't you who took the clock."

"Then where is the clock?" demanded the Headmaster.

"Exactly," said Friday. "Didn't you think it was odd

that Delia didn't have the clock on her, if you thought she was the thief?"

"I assumed she had an accomplice," said the Headmaster, "or she threw it outside into the bushes. The students at this school have a bizarre obsession with throwing things in bushes."

"That is not what happened. The carpet fibers do not support your hypothesis," announced Friday.

"The what?!" exploded the Headmaster. He probably would have lunged for Friday at this point, except he had a heart condition so he didn't think he had the agility to catch an eleven-year-old anymore.

"From my close observation of the carpet fibers, I can see that Delia did indeed go to your desk," said Friday.

"I thought you were going to clear my name!" wailed Delia.

"But she did not go to the front of the desk where the carriage clock was located. No, her size-six Mary Janes went all the way around to the drawers on the other side, where she took your keys so that she could let herself into the kitchen and eat the fresh pastries that had been delivered for this morning's breakfast."

"How on earth can you tell all that from carpet fibers?" demanded the Headmaster.

"I can tell she went to the drawer from the carpet fibers, and I know she took the key because she had it on her when you found her," explained Friday. "And I know she has a great passion for sticky Danishes because even now there are crumbs of flaky pastry about her collar and cuffs."

"Then who did steal the clock and where is it?" asked the Headmaster. "Tell me that if you are so clever."

"You have an excellent cleaner," observed Friday.

"You're not saying it was Manuela?!" gasped the Headmaster. He had a great fondness for his cleaner. She was the only member of the staff who was even more pedantic and grumpy than he was.

"I am observing that she does excellent work," said Friday. "The only reason I could track Delia's movements so accurately across the carpet is because your cleaner has done such a wonderful job of vacuuming. Look at the beautifully precise lines where she vacuums up and down. It's like a football field. You can tell she takes great pride in the accuracy of her corners."

"I can't see her corners," said the Headmaster.

"Exactly," said Friday. "Only a precise expert can turn a vacuum cleaner a hundred and eighty degrees without leaving any pivot marks in the carpet and yet still get the dust out of every corner. She must concentrate very hard on what she is doing, which is how she came to bump your desk."

"What?"

"Look at the deep indentations two inches from each of the feet of your desk," said Friday. "That shows where your desk stood yesterday. She would have been concentrating so hard on your dirty carpet that she inadvertently bumped the desk with her hip. Perhaps because she, too, has been eating too many pastries lately. Really, Headmaster, it is tantamount to entrapment to get a whole shipment of mouthwateringly delicious pastries delivered in the middle of the night. Of course people are going to try to steal them. People think much less rationally at that time, especially when they are hungry from doing all the vacuuming."

"But why did she steal the clock?" asked the Headmaster.

"Manuela didn't steal your clock," said Friday, rolling her eyes. "She bumped your desk with her hip."

"So?" asked the Headmaster.

"That caused the clock to topple off your desk into the bin," said Friday.

"The bin?" said the Headmaster. "But that's not where I keep the bin."

"No, that's where Manuela puts the bin when she is vacuuming, and she didn't hear it fall in because she was listening to Portuguese lessons on her iPod," said Friday.

"How on earth can you know that?" demanded the Headmaster.

"I'll admit that's just a guess," said Friday. "But a guess I am sure is entirely right, because Manuela is not Portuguese."

"What?" blustered the Headmaster.

"She just pretends to be," continued Friday. "I suspect because she is in the witness protection program."

"How could you know that?" asked the Headmaster.

"Because anyone this good at vacuuming," said Friday, "could be earning a six-figure salary working for a very rich person with allergies."

"This is the most ridiculous poppycock I have ever heard," spluttered the Headmaster.

"Really?" said Friday. "But I can prove it all."

"You'll need more than carpet fibers to back you up," said the Headmaster.

"Then how about this?" said Friday as she strode over to the corner of the room where the Headmaster kept his waste-paper bin, reached down through the crumpled papers on the top, and pulled out the carriage clock.

"My clock!" exclaimed the Headmaster.

"As you can see, it stopped at precisely 11:14. That would be when it fell into the bin," said Friday.

"This girl could have staged all this," said the Headmaster, indicating Delia.

"Really?" said Friday. "I've only known her five

minutes, and I know that such a thing would be far beyond the capabilities of her intellect or guile. You've read her report cards. You really should know better."

The Headmaster could see he was beaten. He was not going to get to expel anyone today. It was a shame. Expelling a student always instilled a healthy dose of fear in the other students. And best of all he didn't have to refund the school fees. He had to back out of this situation with his dignity intact. "The girl did still break into my office, steal my keys, and attempt to steal food from the kitchen."

"Surely falsely accusing her of a much greater crime, threatening her with expulsion, and shaming her in the eyes of her family is punishment enough," said Friday. "Besides, it would be dreadful if a story got out to the papers about how Highcrest Academy students are forced to steal food because you don't feed them enough."

"Are you threatening me?" asked the Headmaster.

"I wasn't," admitted Friday. "But now that you've given me the idea, it does sound like a good one."

The Headmaster went red in the face and clenched his fists, but he could not think of what to do, perhaps because anger was making blood rush through his ears and the sound was distracting him.

Suddenly the door burst open and Miss Harrow rushed in.

"What the devil are you interrupting for?" barked the Headmaster.

"I saw it!" exclaimed Miss Harrow. "I was collecting lichen samples in the swamp, when I looked up and saw . . ." Her voice trailed off.

"Saw what?" asked Friday.

"I don't know. He was some sort of savage wild man, half ape or werewolf," said Miss Harrow. "His eyes were terrifying, like those of a swamp yeti!"

"For goodness' sake," said the Headmaster, "you're a scientist. You of all people should know that yetis don't exist. We're trying to clamp down on these fanciful stories before they damage the school's reputation."

"Whatever it was," said Miss Harrow, "it was dangerous."

"It's probably just some older boy trying to scare sixth graders," said the Headmaster.

"That thing was no boy," said Miss Harrow.

The Headmaster sagged. It was bad enough having to deal with students, but hysterical staff and fictional creatures were just too much. He wished he hadn't already eaten the chocolate bar he had snuck into his desk that morning. The Headmaster didn't want to deal with any crisis, but he certainly didn't want to deal with two at a time, so he turned to Delia and Friday.

"Just get out of my office!" he barked at Delia.

"Thank you, sir," said Delia happily.

"But you, Barnes," said the Headmaster.

"Yes, sir?" said Friday.

"Why was it you were sent to me?"

"I hurt my head in an accident with a car and a statue of Socrates," Friday reminded him.

"Oh yes," said the Headmaster. "Are you going to sue the school?"

"No, sir," said Friday.

"Good," said the Headmaster. "Then we needn't talk about it further. I'd like to try to get through the first week of the term without any new lawsuits. Now both of you get out of here."

The two girls turned to leave.

"And, girls," the Headmaster called after them, "I don't want either of you spreading the story of this ridiculous swamp business. Do I make myself clear?"

"Absolutely," said Delia earnestly.

They left, closing the door behind them.

"Thank you," said Friday as she and Delia scuttled away from the office, keen to get as much distance as possible between themselves and the Headmaster in case he changed his mind.

"Why are you thanking me?" asked Delia. "I'm the one who is tremendously grateful to you."

"Yes, but you are the one who got me off for stumbling headfirst into a statue of Socrates," said Friday. "The Headmaster was too distracted by your problem to deal properly with mine."

Delia surprised Friday by wrapping her in a big hug. Friday had not often been hugged in her life. When people in her family hugged it was always an embarrassed and awkward affair, which was brought to an end as quickly as possible. But Delia gave her a good affectionate squeeze.

"I think you're wonderful," announced Delia. "Here's your money."

Friday was so dazed by Delia's unexpected affection that she entirely forgot to complain about the bills coming from inside Delia's sock.

"Now I've got to go and tell my roommate about the swamp yeti," said Delia.

"But you promised you wouldn't tell anyone," Friday reminded her.

"Oh yes, but I can't not tell my roommate," said Delia. "That wouldn't be fair."

Delia hurried off to her own class. Friday looked down at the warm wad of cash in her hand. She had never held so much money in her life. True, she did briefly have $50,000, but that was gone in just a few clicks of a mouse when the money had been electronically transferred to the school. She had never gotten to hold it. There was something so satisfying about having cash money.

As she looked at the money and felt the strange unfamiliar happiness that Delia's affectionate gratitude had given her, Friday had an epiphany. She had spent her whole life accumulating intellectual pursuits, but nothing had made her feel so good as this simple act of helping a schoolmate. She wanted to do it again. Friday saw her destiny before her. She was going to be a private detective. Here she was at Highcrest Academy, surrounded by rich children, and everyone knew rich people had such tremendous problems. If they paid a gardener to do their gardening, a maid to do their cleaning, why not let them pay her to solve their dilemmas?

Friday tucked the money in her own sock, then thought better of it, and tucked it in her pocket (she wasn't a total moral degenerate yet). Then she strode off to find her dorm room with a renewed sense of purpose.

# 10

# Friday's Roommate

Friday had imagined that her dorm would be a long, cold, bleak room with wooden floorboards and steel-framed beds all in a line. (She had read both *Jane Eyre* and the Madeline picture books, so she was well versed on the subject.) When she cautiously pushed open the door Friday was shocked.

For a start there were only two beds, which delighted her—it meant only one person to cope with. Then the room itself was lovely. The carpet was deep thick wool, the kind that made you want

to kick off your shoes and wriggle your toes. The walls were a pleasant creamy yellow. And best of all, the furnishings were stylish yet modern and functional. Friday always enjoyed functional furniture. (Her own chest of drawers back home had been an Edwardian antique. Consequently, on wet days she needed a crowbar to open her sock drawer.) The most beautiful feature of her new dorm room was, however, the window—a huge bay window decorated with leadlight-colored glass and a window seat, and a view across the school's wonderful grounds, the sports fields, the kitchen garden, and, in the distance, the river and the swamp that lay in between.

"Gorgeous!" exclaimed Friday.

"I know," said a girl.

Friday jumped. She hadn't realized there was someone else in the room. "Where did you come from?" asked Friday, spinning around.

"I was hiding in the wardrobe," said the girl. She had a vague and airy way of speaking. "I didn't like to come out until I knew you weren't a dangerous psychopath."

"How do you know I'm not a dangerous psychopath?" asked Friday.

"I don't know," admitted the girl dreamily, "and yet I do. Sorry, I'm not very good at explaining things. My mother says I'm an idiot savant who isn't a savant at anything."

"Your mother says you're an idiot?" Friday's own parents were not in any way affectionate, but even they would not say such a thing about her.

"My mother reads a lot of romance novels," explained the girl calmly. "She likes to think of all the people in her life as characters in novels. That way we can all contribute to her primary narrative of a tortured heroine forced to endure mediocrity by the cruelty of life."

"Is she forced to endure mediocrity?" asked Friday.

"Well, yes," agreed the girl. "But it was her decision to become a real estate agent."

Friday decided it was best to change the subject. "My name is Friday Barnes, and I think I am your roommate."

"Do you realize your name is a day of the week?" asked the girl.

"Yes," said Friday.

"Just checking," said the girl. "I find it very common for girls called Madison to not realize they have been named after the fourth president of the United States."

"What's your name?" asked Friday.

"Me?" asked the girl, as if this was a surprising question. "Melanie Pelly."

"It's a pleasure to meet you," said Friday, shaking Melanie's hand.

"Is it, or are you just saying that out of social convention?" asked Melanie.

Friday considered the question for a moment. "It is," she decided. "I was concerned that you would be narcissistic and ruthless, but you don't appear to be."

"No, they're not my adjectives," agreed Melanie. "I left you the bed by the window because it's nicer, so I thought you'd want it."

"That's very kind," said Friday.

"It makes no difference to me," said Melanie. "I tend to go off wandering in my mind, so it doesn't matter where I am physically. Besides, I can always go and sit on your bed when you're not here, and you'll never know unless I tell you about it."

"True," agreed Friday. "So have you thrown my suitcase into the swamp? I believe that is traditional when a roommate has been delayed."

"Goodness, no," said Melanie. "I did see the other girls dragging some things down there earlier. And I did want to join in so that they would let me be part of the group. But your suitcase was very heavy. So I took my own suitcase and threw that in instead."

"But won't your own things be damaged?" asked Friday.

"I hadn't thought of that," admitted Melanie. "I doubt it. The school doesn't allow personal computers or mobile phones, so there were no electronics in the suitcase. Just a few casual clothes and a hockey stick. I don't mind if the catfish get that."

"Do you know what we do now?" asked Friday.

"Oh yes," said Melanie. "This is my second time here."

"Really?" said Friday, worrying that her roommate was about to tell her that she had attended the school in a previous life when she was Cleopatra.

"I did eight months of seventh grade last year," said Melanie.

"Why only eight months?" asked Friday.

"My family took me on a trip to Africa during spring break," explained Melanie. "I was bitten by a tsetse fly and came down with the sleeping sickness. I only woke up four weeks ago."

"So you're repeating the year?" asked Friday.

"Yes," said Melanie. "Which suits me because I wasn't paying very close attention the first time around."

"Well, according to the schedule our residential tutor gave me, the dinner bell will ring in three minutes," said Friday.

"You'd better use that time to change your clothes, then," said Melanie. "You might put other people off their food if you go to dinner covered in blood."

Friday looked down and realized that her T-shirt and cardigan were spattered in the distinctive reddish brown of drying blood. A wave of nausea swept over her and the floor began to spin.

"Please don't faint," said Melanie, guiding Friday to the bed. "Or if you do, do it on a soft furnishing. If you crack your head open on the nightstand, you'll make a mess of this lovely carpet."

Friday held a hand to her head as if holding her thoughts in and squeezed her eyes shut, willing the dizziness away.

Suddenly the door burst open and a very beautiful

girl strode into the room, flanked by two almost-as-beautiful friends.

"Hello, this is Mirabella Peterson," Melanie told Friday.

"I'm not talking to you," said Mirabella, the very beautiful girl.

"Really?" said Melanie pleasantly. "I could swear I heard sound coming out of your mouth."

Mirabella chose to ignore Melanie and turned to Friday instead. "I don't believe for a second you cut your head open because my father hit your suitcase," Mirabella declared. "I think you had a razor blade hidden in a hairclip and you cut your own head open so you could sue my family. This sort of thing happens all the time. Poor people get the idea from watching too much professional wrestling on television."

"I've got no idea what you're talking about," said Friday. She could barely even hear Mirabella above the swishing nausea-induced sound in her ears.

"This school isn't for the likes of you," said Mirabella. "I've got forty witnesses who will say they saw you leap in front of our car."

"There weren't forty people there," said Melanie. "There were fourteen students, thirteen parents, four chauffeurs, a maiden aunt, two teachers, and Diego the gardener, who was hiding in the bushes staring at Miss Harrow because he is deeply in love with her but doesn't speak English so he can't tell her so."

Everyone looked at Melanie.

"I notice things," she explained. "My brain just does it. The hard part is getting it to notice things that are useful."

Mirabella decided to continue ignoring Melanie and turned back to Friday. "You don't know much about Highcrest, do you?"

"This is my first day," said Friday.

"Well, it is traditional for people like me, who pay full fees, to resent people like you, who don't pay a cent and weasel your way in here on a scholarship," explained the girl. "Every grade has one scholarship student, and it is the Highcrest way to make that student's life here as miserable as possible." Mirabella turned to her friends. "Girls, grab her suitcase. It's going in the swamp."

The two friends grabbed hold of Friday's suitcase, but it didn't budge.

"What are you waiting for?" asked Mirabella.

"It's really heavy," said the friend. "It won't move."

Mirabella walked over and grabbed the handle. "Must I do everything myself?" But she couldn't lift it either. "What have you got in here? Gravel?"

"Books," said Friday.

"Typical. Scholarship kids are always bookworms," said Mirabella. "Well, you haven't heard the last of this. I'm going to make your life here at Highcrest a nightmare."

With that the girls left, slamming the door behind them.

"Why didn't you tell her you're not the scholarship kid?" asked Melanie.

For the third time in the five minutes since she had met her, Friday's roommate had surprised her. "How do you know I'm not?"

"I don't know," said Melanie. "And yet I do. It must be something about your body language."

"I'm not," admitted Friday, "but I didn't like to say so because someone is, and if the scholarship kid really is targeted for bullying, I'm not going to be the one to drop them in it."

"You'll have to put up with a lot yourself," predicted Melanie.

"I'm used to social isolation," said Friday.

"Isolation is nice," agreed Melanie. "That's why people like to go on vacation to deserted beaches. But I don't think what Mirabella has planned for you is going to be anything like that."

# 11

# Bullying

Friday was interested to see how Mirabella intended to make her life miserable. Life at an exclusive boarding school would be a lot more fun than she had imagined if there was a nemesis for her to thwart. But from her brief encounter with Mirabella, Friday doubted that she would be

nemesis-worthy. She was probably going to be more of an annoyance than an archenemy.

And this proved to be correct, because Mirabella's idea of what made someone miserable was wildly different from Friday's. The next morning at nine, when Friday walked into her first class, geography, Mirabella loudly announced, "Attention, everybody, this girl is the scholarship student. Nobody talk to her."

The other students glanced at Friday briefly. None of them had any intention of talking to her anyway. And for Friday this was a dream come true. She wished Mirabella would go to more places with her and make similar announcements, particularly at the hairdresser. Friday had always had tremendously awkward conversations with hairdressers. She found she had a polar-opposite life view to them and, consequently, conversation was painful. She was always embarrassed to confess that she never used a hair dryer. Not on her hair anyway. She often used one as a heat source when accelerating a chemical reaction.

The last person to enter the room was, unprofessionally enough, the teacher. Mr. Maclean was in his early forties. Friday had seen his type before. He had all the confidence and swagger of a man who had spent the first twenty years of his adult life being very good-looking. Now in middle age he had gained a little weight and lost a little hair, and the unnatural confidence seemed slightly pathetic. Even his subject was slightly pathetic. Geography had once been a fascinating noble pursuit. There was a time when the ability to read a contour map, navigate by the stars, predict the weather, and recount the major imports and exports of Guatemala was an impressive skill set. But in this day and age, all these things could be accomplished in three seconds with a smartphone.

Mr. Maclean didn't even seem particularly interested in his own subject. He seemed to want to focus the

beginning of the lesson on dazzling his new students with his charm. While Mr. Maclean told boastful stories about his world travels, Friday took out her first detective novel of the day. She usually read at least one book during the course of the school day, sometimes two, and occasionally three if she had a particularly boring math lesson.

Friday was just getting to a good part in the novel she was reading secretly under the desk when suddenly the door to the classroom burst open and there in the doorway stood . . . a Greek god.

# Chapter

# 12

# The Greek God

Obviously, it was not really a Greek god, because this wasn't Greece and the Greek gods have not paid earthly visits for many centuries now. But the boy who stood in the doorway was totally unearthly in his handsomeness: his hair was so blond, his eyes were so blue, his face was so handsome, and his body was so lean, tall, and athletic. His only blemish was a small vertical scar above his right eyebrow. But even his scar looked handsome, as if

it had been applied by a brilliant Hollywood makeup artist.

Friday found herself wondering if she was having some sort of brain aneurysm, because it was easier to believe she was having an anatomic failure of her cerebellum than to believe that a boy this good-looking could exist.

Then he did the most amazing thing. He smiled, and it was like watching a supernova.

"Sorry, sir, my name is Ian. I'm late because I had a terrible stomachache when I woke up this morning," he said in a beautifully smooth voice.

"Are you all right now?" asked Mr. Maclean, drawing away from this possible source of disease. "Perhaps you should be in bed, resting."

"Oh no," said Ian, smiling warmly at his teacher. "I adore geography. I couldn't stay away."

Ian then turned and looked at Friday, which actually made her flinch. She had seen beautiful people in magazines, but she had never seen someone so good-looking in real life before.

"Are you all right?" whispered Melanie.

"What?" asked Friday. She had forgotten that Melanie was sitting next to her.

"You seem to be hyperventilating," said Melanie, "and given that you had a head injury yesterday, I'm concerned about you."

"I didn't realize seeing someone so good-looking could have such a disconcerting effect on my respiratory system," Friday whispered.

"Who's good-looking?" asked Melanie. She had been staring dreamily out the window. "Oh, you mean Ian Wainscott? Yes, I suppose so. I hadn't really thought about it."

Friday was struggling to not think about it as she watched Ian stride with the confidence of a catwalk model and the athletic grace of a cheetah down the aisle. She gulped. He was coming right toward her. He was looking at her again. Was he going to speak to her?

But Ian simply slid into the desk on the other side of Friday. Friday breathed a quiet sigh of relief and looked down at her empty notebook. Perhaps she would take some geography notes after all to take her mind off this distracting boy.

"Anyway, where was I?" said Mr. Maclean. "Oh yes, explaining the rules. We're stuck with each other for the next twelve months—unless one of you gets expelled." He laughed at his own joke.

"Or you get fired," said Melanie.

Everyone turned and looked at her. "Sorry," said Melanie. "Did I say that out loud? I meant to just think it."

"Yes, anyway," said Mr. Maclean, "I think it's important to start off by knowing where we all stand. A little birdie showed me a copy of your entrance IQ tests this morning."

This got everyone's attention. Mr. Maclean smirked at the class, very pleased with himself for catching their focus. People loved knowing their IQ score. If it was high, that was obviously good. But if it was low, that was good, too, because they could tell themselves they were too smart for their intelligence to register on a standardized examination.

"We are indeed privileged to have the brightest student this year right here in our class," said Mr. Maclean mysteriously.

But it was apparently not a mystery to the majority of students, because they all turned and looked at Ian. Ian smiled. He was better at smiling than Mr. Maclean. His smile had only the slightest trace of smugness in it.

"Yes, we all know," said Mirabella. "Ian is a genius. He was always winning all the prizes at school."

"Ian who?" said Mr. Maclean, checking his register. "Wainscott? Oh no, not him. He's second. The brightest student this year—indeed, ever to take the Highcrest Academy IQ test—is a boy called . . . Friday Balmes."

Friday could feel the heat rising up through her neck.

"Who?" asked Ian, visibly shocked. Angry even.

"Friday Balmes," said Mr. Maclean.

Friday could not see her face, but she was entirely sure that if she could it would be beetroot-red at this moment.

"Balmes, put your hand up," ordered Mr. Maclean, looking around the room.

There was no escaping now. Given time, Friday could have forged a birth certificate, a passport, and school documents and passed herself off under another name—Adrianna Hicklestein, for instance—but she could not do that in a split second, and certainly not without access to Photoshop software and a color printer. She would have to say something.

"Barnes," she said.

"No, Balmes," corrected Mr. Maclean.

"I think I know my own name," said Friday.

"It's you?" said Mr. Maclean, clearly surprised. He

squinted at Friday. He had not noticed her before. "You're not a boy, are you? I thought Friday was a boy's name."

Some of the class giggled. Mortification sank into every cell in Friday's body.

"My name is Friday Barnes," said Friday. "Should you be wearing reading glasses, Mr. Maclean?"

"No, no," said Mr. Maclean. "My eyesight is twenty-twenty." He squinted at the register, holding it as far away as possible. "Ah yes, Barnes, you're right. Must have been a typo. Sorry, I thought you'd be a boy. And taller."

"I'm not," said Friday.

"Evidently," agreed Mr. Maclean. "Anyway, Barnes here is the new top dog. He is—I mean, *she* is your competition for the next twelve months. The one you've got to take down if you want to be the alpha student."

"Surely education should be a collaborative learning process, not a dog-eat-dog competition?" queried Friday.

This time the whole class laughed, including Mr. Maclean.

"My dear girl," said Mr. Maclean, "this is a private school. You've entered *Lord of the Flies* now."

The rest of the lesson went smoothly enough. Mirabella took every opportunity to make snide comments about Friday, but she was obviously having difficulty arousing the interest of the other students. When they did glance at Friday it was with apathetic disinterest, which was just the way Friday liked things.

"Excuse me," said Ian.

Friday looked up and flinched again. Ian had leaned across the aisle and had his hand on the edge of her desk. He smiled his supernova smile and she caught her breath. Somewhere in the back of her very large brain Friday noted that Ian even smelled nice.

"May I borrow a pen?" asked Ian. "I seem to have forgotten mine."

"Of course," said Friday. "Help yourself." She gestured toward the pencil box at the corner of her desk. Ian took a pen and went back to his work, studiously taking notes as the lesson progressed. After a while Friday found she could concentrate sufficiently to draw a diagram of the ecosystem of a rainforest. Everything was proceeding normally enough when suddenly her pencil box imploded.

Now, I know explosions are much more common

than implosions, so you may be struggling to imagine what this would look like. So here is precisely what happened: The pink plastic pencil box on the corner of Friday's desk suddenly crumpled in on itself, like an aluminum can being crushed underfoot. The pencil box then proceeded to ooze a liquid, which puddled underneath, then started to eat through the desk while bubbling, hissing, and billowing blue smoke.

"That's an interesting pencil box," said Melanie. "Where did you get it?"

"I didn't do it!" exclaimed Friday, which we know is what all perpetrators of crimes say.

"Stop it, stop this at once!" demanded the openly hostile Mr. Maclean, as if Friday had the power to control the now-quite-advanced chemical reaction. The whole class gathered around Friday's desk, watching the puddle of molten plastic and floating pencils sizzle and pop until the acid ate right through Friday's desk and everything dropped onto the carpet.

All the girls, and several of the less image-conscious boys, screamed. And Mr. Maclean, finally in an act of good sense, ordered everyone out into the corridor, which was a good thing because as the acid started to eat the carpet, the synthetic fibers were giving off a toxic gas. If there had been a canary in the room, it would have perished instantly.

Out in the corridor, Friday felt ill—and not from the effect of inhaling poisonous gas.

"You look pale and clammy," Melanie observed.

"I think I'm in shock," said Friday, taking her pulse to gain further data. "Changing schools is bad enough, but getting hit by a car yesterday and now this? I'm not used to things happening to me. I'm used to watching things happen to other people."

"I think you're about to have something else happen to you," said Melanie, nodding toward the classroom door, where Mr. Maclean was emerging, the last to leave. He closed the door firmly behind him. He had soot on his suit jacket and he was clearly very angry about it. Mr. Maclean looked about and spotted Friday. He strode over.

"You, go and see the Headmaster at once," ordered Mr. Maclean.

"But I didn't do anything," declared Friday.

Mr. Maclean ignored her. He had taken a booklet of detention slips out of his pocket and was angrily writing on one.

"I'd hardly turn my own pencil box into a bomb," argued Friday.

"I have taught at this school for seventeen years," said Mr. Maclean, not looking up as he continued to write. His angry message to the Headmaster about Friday was clearly a long one. "It never ceases to amaze me what overprivileged children will do to draw attention to themselves."

"She isn't overprivileged," said Mirabella. "She's the scholarship girl."

This made Mr. Maclean look up from his note. He looked Friday up and down. "Yes, that would explain a great deal as well."

"But-but-but," spluttered Friday, completely belying the fact that she had won the Agatha Higgenbottom Award for Spontaneous Public Speaking just the previous year. But that is what happens when you go into shock.

"Go!" ordered Mr. Maclean, thrusting the small yellow note at Friday.

Friday took the note and looked at it. Her teacher's handwriting really was dreadful, but she correctly judged that now was not the time to point that out. Friday sighed, suppressing the welling urge to burst into tears, which was no doubt symptomatic of shock as well. It was ridiculous to cry over such a patently false accusation. But it did hurt. The accusation made her sick to her stomach. And having read several dozen books on psychology, she knew that even if she were able to confront Mr. Maclean with conclusive forensic proof that the culprit was not her, Mr. Maclean would still never again see her in the same light.

Friday blinked once, then realized the whole class was watching to see what she would do, so she held her head high and turned to leave. The tight knot of students parted for her as she started down the long empty corridor, until one voice called her back.

"Friday?"

Friday turned. It was Ian, the beautifully beautiful boy. He smiled at her. Then held something out. It was her pen. "Would you like your pen back?" She looked at the pen, then at Ian's face. His smile was not beautiful anymore. It was evil and knowing. Instantly, she knew Ian had done it. He had imploded her pencil box.

"Friday Barnes!" yelled Mr. Maclean. "Do I have to give you another detention slip?"

"No," said Friday, her eyes still locked with Ian's. She reached out and took the pen. After all, it was the only one she had now, and it would be silly to let him keep it. She needed something to write with.

If she had been a great wit, Friday would have thought of some pithy remark to put this boy in his place or to warn him that he had met his match. But Friday had always found that threats were useless. If you are going to hit someone, it's much better not to tell them about it first. And she could not think of any words adequate to convey how she felt about this bafflingly random attack on her stationery collection. She knew private schools were competitive, but to destroy her pencil case just because she scored higher than him in an IQ test seemed astonishingly extreme.

Friday turned and headed to the Headmaster's office. It was a slow walk of shame, every footstep echoing on the cold linoleum floor.

# 13

# The Swamp

The rest of the day passed smoothly enough. Friday didn't have any more classes with Ian Wainscott. And despite Mirabella's best efforts, having her pencil box implode seemed to give Friday a greater sense of credibility among her fellow students.

In the corridors, people whispered about her as she walked past. A few pointed and sniggered. But they didn't snigger too loudly. It would be foolish

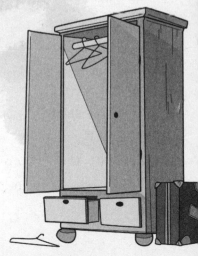

to snigger at someone with knowledge of destructive chemicals.

And so her first week at Highcrest Academy went by. Friday had not achieved her aim of going unnoticed and ignored by everyone. But she found this was something she could cope with. After the last class of the week, Friday was tired and emotionally exhausted as she returned to her dorm room with Melanie.

When she opened the door she met an unexpected sight. All the drawers and doors of her wardrobe were open, and there was nothing inside.

"Oh dear," said Melanie. "It looks like they got you."

Friday surprised herself with her own emotional reaction. Her eyes started to prickle and her stomach felt like it had been squeezed. She was not normally an emotional girl, so for her it was upsetting to be upset.

"Don't take it personally," said Melanie, noticing Friday's face crumple. "They do it to all people who are different."

Friday sniffed.

"It'll be all right," said Melanie. "I'll come with you down to the swamp and help you find which bush they threw your clothes in. You never have to look too far. The kids here are pretty lazy. They always just throw them in one of the first bushes they see."

"It's not that," said Friday, although it was a little bit that. "It's just that I feel violated to know that someone has been through my things. My private things."

"You mean your brown cardigan collection?" asked Melanie. "Maybe it's for the best. You probably shouldn't be so emotionally attached to knitwear."

"I like my brown cardigans," said Friday, a tear actually escaping and running down her cheek. She had never had a teddy bear, a security blanket, or emotionally supportive parents. Her cardigans had, for many years, been the most comforting thing in her life.

"Okay," said Melanie. "We'll find them, I promise."

She really was a very good friend.

If you didn't mind the smell or having muddy shoes, the swamp wasn't really too dreadful a place. In fact, if you had called it a natural waterbird habitat, you could have charged birdwatchers admission and turned it into a tourist destination. But school students are not so philosophical about their environment. To them, a swamp is a swamp and a stink is a stink, no matter how pretty the birds are or how interesting the root system of the water lily is.

Friday's clothes were not immediately evident on the outskirts of the swamp, where Melanie had thought they would be.

"This is the problem with having camouflaged clothes," said Friday. "They are difficult to find when you lose them."

"Only in a swamp," said Melanie. "They'd be easy to see somewhere bright like the surface of the sun."

"They'd burn on the surface of the sun," observed Friday.

"Yes," agreed Melanie. "Which would probably be a good thing."

There was a complicated maze of paths that led through the swamp down to the estuary that marked the edge of the school's land. But since Melanie and Friday didn't know where they were going they just wandered aimlessly.

"This is hopeless," said Friday. "They could be any-where. The swamp must cover fifty acres. We'll never be able to search all that."

"You should trust in fate to lead you to your clothes,"

said Melanie. "If you are meant to have them back, then you will find them."

"You think an existential force will lead me to my clothes?" asked Friday.

"Not really," admitted Melanie. "I doubt an existential force likes looking at your brown cardigans either."

Suddenly a figure burst out of the bushes and slammed straight into the girls, knocking them to the ground, which was especially unpleasant because the ground was muddy.

"I'm terribly sorry!"

The girls looked up to see Miss Harrow standing over them, carrying a brown leather suitcase.

"I didn't see you there," continued Miss Harrow.

"There are a lot of blind turns in this swamp," agreed Melanie. "We didn't see you either."

"I was just collecting samples of phytoplankton for next week's lesson on single-cell organisms," said Miss Harrow.

"Really?" said Friday. She liked single-cell organisms. "Will we be studying zooplankton as well?"

"I thought we could work up to zooplankton for next term," said Miss Harrow.

"I shall look forward to that," said Friday. "My parents wouldn't let me keep zooplankton in our house, ever since my father drank my specimen, thinking it was a glass of water, and ended up in the hospital with raging gastroenteritis."

"I'd better be getting along," said Miss Harrow. "Don't stay out too long, girls. It'll be dark soon. You don't want to get lost in the swamp at night. It's fascinating by day, but quite unpleasant in the dark."

Miss Harrow left and the girls kept walking.

"I wonder why Miss Harrow was lying," pondered Melanie.

"What?" asked Friday.

"I'm pretty good at telling when people are lying," explained Melanie. "I think it's because I don't listen to anything they say."

"But why would she lie about us studying plankton?" asked Friday.

All of a sudden Friday and Melanie were knocked over again.

"*¡Lo siento, lo siento!*" said Diego, apologizing profusely as he helped the girls up.

"It's all right," said Friday. "No harm done."

*"Discúlpeme,"* said Diego, barely paying attention as he hurried off in the direction Miss Harrow had taken.

"How peculiar," said Friday as she watched him go.

"Love does that to a man," said Melanie. "He's always lurking in bushes as he follows Miss Harrow around. They say that Latin Americans are a very passionate people."

"Who says?" asked Friday.

"All the romance novels I've ever read," said Melanie. "Oh look! Your clothes."

Friday looked in the direction Melanie was pointing. She could see her clothes, which were neatly folded on top of a channel marker, fifty yards out into the estuary.

"How good are you at swimming?" asked Melanie.

"I'm okay at breaststroke and backstroke," said Friday, "because they're the ones where you don't have to put your face in the water."

"I would offer to swim out and fetch them for you," said Melanie, "but I don't want to."

"I understand," said Friday. "And even if I swam out there, I'd have to climb the channel marker. The clothes must be five yards above the waterline."

"What is that written on the channel marker?" asked Melanie.

Friday peered across the water. Her eyesight was not good; too many books read by flashlight under the covers for that. But now that Melanie had pointed it out she could make out some letters on the thick vertical pole.

2
FB
FRM
IFW

"What does that mean?" asked Melanie.

"To Friday Barnes from Ian Wainscott," said Friday. "He has inexplicably attacked my possessions again."

"Of course," said Melanie. "I knew he was in love with you."

"Humph," scoffed Friday. There was not a real word that could adequately convey her feelings.

"I suppose we could ask Diego to take out a dinghy and a long rake and get them down for you," said Melanie.

Friday looked at her clothes as if seeing them for the first time. "No, let's not bother," she said. "They are pretty dreadful, aren't they?"

"I didn't like to say so, but yes," agreed Melanie.

"Delia Michaels gave me five hundred dollars for helping her to not be expelled," said Friday. "I'll use that to buy some new clothes."

"How?" asked Melanie. "We aren't allowed into town, and besides it's twenty-five miles away. We aren't allowed Internet access either, so we can't shop online."

"I've got a ham radio," said Friday. "I'll call my uncle Bernie and get him to drop off a delivery."

"Does your Uncle Bernie have good taste in clothes?" asked Melanie.

"No, but he probably has better taste than me," admitted Friday.

# Chapter
# 14
# Fisticuffs

Friday and Melanie made their way out of the swamp and were walking across the hockey field. They were not walking quickly because they were returning to their room to do homework. And the feet always move slower when the brain does not really want to get to its destination.

"Mel!" came a voice from up ahead.

The girls looked up to see a large athletic boy thundering down the side of the field toward them.

"Oh, Mel, I'm so glad to see you,"

puffed the large boy. He bent over, his hands on his knees, as he tried to catch his breath.

"This is my brother Binky. He's a sophomore," explained Melanie.

"Hello," said Binky. He was clearly as amiable as his sister, although enormous and muscly like someone who plays a great deal of football, which he did.

"Are you quite all right?" asked Friday.

"Oh yes. I mean, no," said Binky. "I'm in kind of a mess, in fact. That's why I came running to find Mel. She's the brains in the family. Thought she might know what to do."

"You're the brains in the family?" asked Friday.

"Yes," said Melanie. "You should meet my other brothers."

"Dim bulbs," explained Binky.

Melanie nodded as though this was an indisputable truth.

"So what sort of trouble are you in?" asked Friday.

"Oh yes," said Binky, who'd clearly forgotten what he was talking about. "I'm in a fight."

"But you're here," said Melanie.

"No, I mean I'm scheduled to be in a fight," said

Binky. "I've got to go and fight with Simmons the senior at four o'clock behind the boys' locker rooms."

"Why?" asked Friday.

"I had an assignment to hand in to Mr. Maclean," explained Binky. "Simmons asked me to hand in his as well. But he says I forgot."

"Did you forget?" asked Friday.

"No, at least I don't think I did," said Binky. "No, I definitely didn't. Because I handed mine in at the same time. And Mr. Maclean got that all right. But he docked Simmons's grade, saying his assignment was two days late."

"How curious," said Friday.

"Anyway," continued Binky, "he told me he was going to give me a darn good thrashing and I was to meet him at four o'clock to get it."

"So how do you want Melanie to help you?" asked Friday.

"I hadn't thought that far," admitted Binky. "I knew I should ask her for advice. But if I knew what the advice was, I wouldn't have had to run here, would I?"

"So," said Friday, turning to Melanie.

"So what?" asked Melanie.

"Do you have any advice?" asked Friday.

"No," said Melanie.

"Oh dear," said Binky.

"Except," said Melanie.

"Yes?" said Binky hopefully.

"You could ask Friday to help," said Melanie.

Melanie and Binky turned to look at Friday.

"Why are you looking at me?" asked Friday. "I know absolutely nothing about physical violence."

"But you're very good at solving mysteries and problems," said Melanie.

"But this isn't a mystery or a problem," said Friday. "It is simply a fact. Your brother is going to get beaten up."

"Sounds like a problem to me," said Binky.

"But what do you expect me to do about it?" asked Friday. "I'm only five feet tall. And I'm in an emotionally fragile state because my entire collection of brown cardigans has just been lost at sea."

"I'm sure you'll think of something," said Melanie. "You're tremendously clever. Even though you're not the scholarship girl."

"She's not? Then who is?" said Binky.

"It's a mystery," said Melanie.

"But if she's not the scholarship girl," said Binky, "why does she wear those dreadful cardigans?"

"That's also a mystery," said Melanie.

"It is not a mystery," protested Friday. "It is a perfectly rational fashion choice."

"Oh dear," said Melanie, checking her watch. "It's three minutes to four, so if Binky doesn't appear behind the boys' locker rooms in the next one hundred and eighty seconds, he's going to get beaten up for not turning up for his beating."

"Really?" said Binky. "If I'd known I was going to get in a fight today, I would have worn my watch."

So they all hurried off to the boys' locker rooms. It was an unattractive brown building that smelled unpleasant. The locker rooms were built into the slope on the side of the football field, so even though the building was single-story at the front, it was two-story at the back, which provided a large double wall to shield would-be pugilists from the eyes of the teaching staff.

When Friday, Binky, and Melanie arrived, Simmons was already there. He was a tall, slim boy and, unlike Binky, he seemed to have his wits about him. He had brought along a dozen friends and boxing enthusiasts. No doubt he was confident of a victory and wanted plenty of witnesses.

Simmons had already taken off his jacket and was rolling his shoulders, warming up so that he didn't strain himself in the imminent thrashing.

"What do I do?" asked Binky in a whisper to Friday.

"Take off your jacket, too," said Friday. "It will buy us some time to think."

"It's a shame we're not allowed cell phones," said Melanie. "We could have called Daddy's helicopter and gotten him to airlift you out of here."

"Your father has a helicopter?" asked Friday.

"Oh yes, he hates being stuck in traffic," said Melanie.

"I suppose the ambulance service might airlift me out of here if my injuries are serious enough," said Binky, cheering up at the idea. He liked a good ride. He proceeded to roll up his sleeves, which took a while because his forearms were very large.

"Okay," said Binky. "Now what do I do?"

"Traditionally, in amateur fights you have to step closer to your opponent so that you can taunt and belittle him," said Friday.

"Why?" asked Binky. "That doesn't sound very nice."

"It's more to psych yourself up," said Friday. "So you can bring yourself to hit him."

"So running isn't an option?" asked Binky.

"There are twelve of them and only one of you," said Friday. "Unless you are incredibly good at running, there's little point."

"I'm not fast at anything with my feet or my brain," said Binky. He stepped forward and Simmons did the same.

"You need to learn a lesson," said Simmons. "You need to learn respect for your elders and betters."

"Really?" said Binky. He was getting confused (a common problem for him). "I thought you were mad because you got a D on your assignment."

"Don't answer back to me," said Simmons, who was now pointing his finger at Binky's face.

As Simmons took two steps forward, Friday watched him closely.

"Binky!" called Friday. "I know what you should do!"

"You do?" said Binky. "Thank goodness."

"From the way he is standing I can tell that Simmons has a recurrent knee injury in his right leg, and given his lanky frame and this school's emphasis on competitive sports, it's probably from too much high-jump practice," said Friday. "And he has a distaste for violence, because he is taking a long time to get around to hitting you."

"I am not," objected Simmons.

"Binky, the key to all martial arts is compromising your opponent's balance," said Friday. "Don't think. Sweep his right leg!"

Binky did as he was told. Not thinking was his strength. He leaped onto his left foot and swung his right foot forward to knock the other boy's foot from underneath him.

"Ow!" cried Simmons as he fell on the ground.

"You won!" cried Melanie delightedly.

"You cheated," accused Simmons as he writhed in pain on the floor.

"I don't see how that can be the case," said Binky. "I only did as I was told."

"Binky, I said *his* right," chided Friday. "Not *your* right. You swept his left leg. Now he'll have two knee injuries."

"Oh dear," said Binky. He bent over Simmons and apologized sincerely. "Terribly sorry about that. Never been good with left and right."

"It doesn't matter, Binky," said Melanie. "It worked. It's the thought that counts."

"I didn't know I'd had a thought," said Binky. "I'm glad it was a good one."

"Let that be a lesson to you," said Friday, addressing Simmons, who was still writhing on the ground. "All fist fighting is stupid. You have to use your hands to do any number of important things: write, play piano, catch a ball . . ."

"Pick your nose," added Binky.

"Yes, even pick your nose," agreed Friday.

The other seniors had gathered around their friend, unsure of what to do. They were a little embarrassed because Simmons appeared to be crying.

"Maybe we should leave before any of the other seniors decide they want to hit Binky," suggested Melanie.

"All right," agreed Friday. "So I declare this fight to be officially over."

"But my paper!" protested Simmons. "Because of him I got a D for handing it in late. If I don't maintain a C average, I get thrown off the lacrosse team."

"Really?" said Friday. "I didn't know it was that easy to get excluded from sports."

"Only from varsity teams," said Melanie. "If you're not on a team, they still make you do some sort of exercise, such as running around a field. Or worse . . . aerobics."

Friday shuddered.

"I'm the captain of the team!" exclaimed Simmons. "I can't get thrown off."

Friday felt a twinge of sympathy. She couldn't empathize with someone wanting to play sports. But she understood not wanting to let people down. This was an Achilles heel for her as well. And seeing Simmons on the floor, clutching his knee and struggling not to cry in front of his friends did make Friday feel guilty.

"Don't worry," said Friday. "I'll investigate this matter for you. If Binky says he handed your assignment in on time—"

"And I did," said Binky.

"Then I believe him," continued Friday. "Because, no offense to Binky, but I don't think he has the intelligence to lie."

"I don't," agreed Binky. "And no offense taken."

"There is more to this, and I promise to get to the bottom of it for you," said Friday to Simmons, "on the condition that you must never challenge Binky to a fight again, because he is a large simple boy who can, when given the proper instruction by me, hurt you seriously. Let's go."

The study hall bell rang. All the students scuttled off in different directions except for Simmons, who hobbled between two friends.

"Thank you so much," said Binky as he, Melanie, and Friday turned back to the dorms.

"That's all right," said Friday. "Anything for Melanie's brother."

"How much do I owe you?" asked Binky.

"Owe?" asked Friday. "Nothing at all."

"I heard how Delia paid you to get her off that stealing charge," said Binky. "I don't want to be a cheapskate. I'll pay the going rate."

"Delia paid her five hundred dollars," said Melanie. "Do you even have five hundred dollars, Binky?"

"Goodness no," said Binky. "But I'm sure I've got something you'd like."

"She's not going to want your Xbox or your PlayStation," said Melanie. "Friday is an intellectual."

"I don't know about that," said Friday. "I like Wii. I like it when an avatar does things for me."

"I know!" exclaimed Binky. "I'll give you a baseball bat!"

"But I don't play!" Friday said. "Not any sport. My parents are both academics. The only good thing they ever did for me was write a note to my school saying they refused to let me participate in any body-contact sport, ball sport, or cardiovascular exercise because it violated their academic principles."

"No, no, no," said Binky. "Not that type of bat. You'd never play with it. It's an autographed bat, signed by Babe Ruth."

"That sounds valuable," said Friday. "I couldn't take that from you."

"It's okay," said Binky cheerfully. "I've got two. Uncle Henry got me one for Christmas, and forgot that he'd already gotten me one for my birthday."

"But still, Binky—" said Friday.

"I won't take no for an answer," said Binky. "Baseball bats can be totally useful to have around. Apart from playing baseball, they're handy if you need to hammer a nail into the wall or squash a cockroach without getting goo on your best shoes. Or you could take it with you if you go walking in the swamp again."

"Why?" asked Friday.

"You might need it to bop that yeti fellow on the head," said Binky earnestly as he ran off to his dorm.

Melanie and Friday kept walking.

"I like your brother," said Friday.

"Yes," agreed Melanie. "He's just like a big puppy. Except that you don't have to clean up his poop or take him for walks. So really he's even better than a puppy."

# Chapter
## 15
## The Stakeout

And so the following Monday, at nine, Friday and Melanie left the breakfast hall and headed in the opposite direction to the sports fields.

"What will we say when Miss Spitzer catches us skipping PE?" asked Melanie.

"She'll be angry, but I doubt she'll report us," said Friday. "I think on some level Miss Spitzer will be secretly

relieved. It can't be fun trying to teach people like us to have hand-eye coordination."

Friday and Melanie entered the administration block. The social studies staff room was in the west wing, just along the corridor from the Headmaster's office. There was no one in the staff room when they arrived.

"What do we do now?" asked Melanie. "Should we hide in a closet?"

"I find it is usually better to hide in plain sight," said Friday. "It's very hard to explain your way out of being in a closet. But when someone realizes that you shouldn't be sitting right in front of them, and yet you have been sitting right in front of them for some time, they never make as much fuss."

So Friday and Melanie sat down on the now familiar bench outside the Headmaster's office. Friday noted that the Headmaster had changed the lock on his door. The new lock had a fingerprint recognition keypad. Friday shook her head at the foolishness. Fingerprint technology was even easier to overcome than a tumbler lock. The Headmaster obviously did not go to the movies very often. If he did he would be more reluctant to use a technology that was traditionally overcome by cutting a person's thumb off.

"Now what?" asked Melanie.

"We eat," said Friday as she took out her snack food. "I've got a sandwich bag full of guacamole in one pocket, corn chips in the other, and some superhot chili sauce hidden inside my fountain pen."

"That'll be handy," remarked Melanie. "If we don't eat the sauce, you can use it as a weapon."

They had been there just thirty-four minutes when they heard the *swoosh* and the pneumatic hiss of the main door opening as Miss Priddock, the school secretary, entered. She was a tall blond woman wearing a bright red blouse. She noticed the girls and smiled at them, then went behind her desk and set to work. Friday and Melanie could not see what she was doing because receptionists' desks are always slightly too high. This is so that the receptionist will not accidentally make eye contact and, therefore, socially awkward small talk with anyone waiting for an appointment. As such, the girls could only see the top of her perfectly arranged blond hair.

"What's she doing?" whispered Melanie.

"If I was being charitable I would say she is browsing through an office supply catalog," whispered Friday. "But I think more realistically she is probably flicking through a gossip magazine and eating a chocolate cookie."

"How can you tell?" asked Melanie.

"You can hear her turning the pages," said Friday. "From the sound, you can tell it is lightweight paper, therefore not a book, but glossy, therefore not a newspaper. Lightweight glossy paper is used in the type of large stationery catalog present in the desk drawers of all secretaries. It is also used in gossip magazines. And since this woman does not look like the type of person who enjoys browsing for office supplies—"

"Oh, I do," interrupted Melanie. "There is something very satisfying about choosing notepads and erasers."

"I agree," said Friday. "But some people are more superficial."

"How can you tell she's eating a chocolate cookie?" asked Melanie.

"The sound and speed of her chomps," explained Friday. "The chocolate coating muffles the chomping sound. And if she were eating a plain old graham cracker she would just eat it. But a chocolate cookie is something to be savored and enjoyed. On average, people eat chocolate cookies forty-three percent slower than non-chocolate cookies, and even slower than that if they just had a big meal and aren't terribly hungry."

Their conversation was interrupted as the door sucked open again and two teachers entered, heading toward the pigeonholes where the Highcrest faculty members picked up their daily mail. One of the teachers was an older harried man in a tweed suit and blue bow tie.

"That's Mr. Braithwaite," said Melanie. "He teaches ancient history."

The second teacher was Mr. Maclean.

"There he is," said Melanie.

"Hmm," said Friday. She was concentrating intently on his behavior.

Mr. Braithwaite ignored Miss Priddock and the girls and walked directly to his pigeonhole while staring at the ground and muttering to himself. But Mr. Maclean looked around, saw Miss Priddock, and smiled.

Friday's eyes narrowed. "Did you see that?" she whispered to Melanie.

"What?" asked Melanie. She had been staring at the potted plant in the corner and doubted that was what Friday was referring to.

"His smile," said Friday. "I have cataloged 1,028 different types of human smiles, and that smile falls into a very specific subcategory of smiles that can only be achieved by practicing while looking in the mirror."

"Practicing what?" asked Melanie.

"Practicing handsomeness," said Friday. "Mr. Maclean has spent hours and hours of his life looking in the mirror and smiling to see what he has to do to make his smile look as handsome as possible."

"How peculiar," said Melanie. She found it hard to concentrate on anything for prolonged periods of time, certainly not her own face.

"And look at the state of his shoes," continued Friday. Mr. Maclean had a thick Plimsoll line of black mud around the soles of his tan boat shoes. Friday

was several yards away, but she still leaned toward them and sniffed. "He's been doing something in the swamp."

"Miss Priddock," said Mr. Maclean, "looking fabulous today, I see."

Miss Priddock giggled and smiled her own less practiced yet equally nauseating smile back.

Mr. Maclean sauntered over to the pigeonholes, unlocked his, swung the little door open, and reached up to get his papers, but as he put his hand in, he turned and spoke once more to Miss Priddock.

"I was observing the topography of the moon's

surface last night, and I thought of you," said Mr. Maclean.

Miss Priddock giggled again.

"Such beauty outshining all others," said Mr. Maclean. He smiled again, but this time it was a different type of affected smile, more serious and suggestive.

"I think I'm going to be sick," whispered Melanie.

Miss Priddock just giggled.

Mr. Maclean laughed as well. He scraped the papers out of his pigeonhole without looking and walked off to his office.

"That is disappointing," said Friday.

"It is?" said Melanie.

"I was hoping it would take longer to solve this case," said Friday with a sigh as she got to her feet. "Now we have no excuse. We will have to go back and do the rest of PE."

"Oh dear," said Melanie. "And at such short notice. There's no time for us to come down with a life-threatening contagious disease. Are you absolutely sure you solved the problem?"

"I'm afraid so," said Friday. "Come on, we'll walk slowly. But I need to talk to Miss Priddock first." Friday leaned over the receptionist's counter and saw that she had been quite right. Miss Priddock was reading a gossip magazine. "Excuse me, I'd like to make an appointment to see the Headmaster."

"The earliest I can squeeze you in is ten o'clock tomorrow," said Miss Priddock.

"There's no chance we could see him right now?" asked Friday.

"He's got another appointment," said Miss Priddock.

"Of course," said Friday. "I had observed that on the third Tuesday of the month the Headmaster's hair is always impeccably black. So the third Monday of the month is when he gets his roots dyed."

Miss Priddock gasped. "How did you know? I was sworn to secrecy."

"And I assume he has to drive sixty miles away for the appointment," said Friday, "so there is no chance he'll bump into anyone from school."

"No," said Miss Priddock. "Actually he has a boat hidden in the swamp. He takes a forty-minute trip up the river."

"Intriguing," said Friday. "There is a lot of coming and going from the school swamp."

"He's so vain," continued Miss Priddock, leaning in to whisper conspiratorially. "He's always going on about being on a diet. But a number of times I've caught him secretly gobbling a chocolate bar. And last week a lemon tart went missing off my desk. I swear it was him."

"Interesting," said Friday as she turned and left with Melanie.

"What's interesting?" asked Melanie. "The stuff about the Headmaster eating chocolate or the fact that Miss Priddock is wildly indiscreet?"

"Both," said Friday.

So Friday and Melanie went back to their PE class. Mercifully, when they got there Vanessa Dieppe had broken her nose playing dodgeball, so they got to spend the rest of the class standing around waiting for the ambulance to arrive while Miss Spitzer tried to pretend she wasn't having a panic attack as she imagined the inevitable lawsuit from the girl's parents.

# 16

# The Sticky Substance

Friday and Melanie returned to sit on the bench out-

side the Headmas-
ter's office at ten the
following morning.
Friday had told Sim-
mons to meet them
there. He'd arrived
first because he
didn't want his limp
to make him late.

"Do you have proof
of my innocence?"
asked Simmons.

"No," said Friday, "but we will soon."

The Headmaster did not make them wait too long this time. It was just eight minutes past ten when he emerged from his office and saw the three students sitting there.

"You," said the Headmaster uncivilly as he eyed Friday. "I saw your name on my schedule and I had hoped it was a mistake."

"No mistake," said Friday. "We needed to meet with you to redress an injustice suffered by Simmons!"

Simmons nodded.

"Shall we come into your office, or would you like to conduct the meeting out here?" asked Friday. "We don't mind waiting while you fetch yourself a chocolate cookie."

"A chocolate coo—" the Headmaster began to splutter, but then he gave up. "How on earth did you know that was what I was after?"

"I've done a statistical analysis of the amount of time you make people wait before they come in to see you," said Friday. "Parents are left to wait three minutes, teachers six minutes, and students seventeen. No doubt this is a Sun Tzu's *Art of War*-inspired intimidation tactic they teach you at headmaster training camp. So the question was, What would make you emerge from your office nine minutes before your self-imposed schedule? You don't have the uncomfortable look of someone who needs to use the bathroom—"

"Oh dear," said Melanie. "I don't like to think about the Headmaster as being someone who uses the bathroom."

"But it is just after ten," continued Friday, "which means it is three hours since you ate breakfast, so you are probably getting peckish, and you are an intelligent, observant man—"

"Thank you for noticing," said the Headmaster sarcastically.

"So, like me," Friday went on, "you would have noticed that Miss Priddock has an open packet of chocolate cookies sitting on her desk. You have probably been thinking about those chocolate cookies for the last hour, knowing you shouldn't eat one because you must be familiar with the heart attack statistics for overweight men in their sixties with stressful jobs. You would also be deterred by the fact that you would have to smile and be nice to Miss Priddock. Not a pleasant experience for a man of your stature, especially since she accused you of stealing her lemon tart last week. So it would have taken you a full sixty-eight minutes for your hunger to overwhelm your dignity, by which time you were so brain-addled with chocolate-longing that you forgot I would be sitting here."

"Sometimes I wonder if you are startlingly gifted," said the Headmaster, "or you simply have access to some sort of illicit counterintelligence mind-reading device."

"It is all just a matter of simple observation," said Friday. "But rest assured, you won't have to demean yourself to Miss Priddock. I took the liberty of bringing two chocolate cookies with me."

Friday produced a sandwich bag holding two cookies.

"Is this a bribe?" asked the Headmaster.

"Not at all," said Friday. "I simply don't want you to be making the decision you are about to make in a hypoglycemic state."

The Headmaster looked at the chocolate cookies. They were the good kind, with a thick layer of chocolate on the outside and another layer of chocolate cream in the middle. "All right," he said, giving up and taking a bite as he led the three students into his office. "What's this all about, then?"

"We have to wait for one more person to arrive," said Friday.

"Will that person be bringing me chocolate cookies as well?" asked the Headmaster, half sarcastically and half hopefully.

"No," said Friday. "Although I bet he smarms one off Miss Priddock."

They heard the opening *swoosh* of the external door and the pneumatic hiss as it slowly retracted.

"This will be him," said Friday.

"Good morning, Miss Priddock," said Mr. Maclean.

"Maclean," groaned the Headmaster. "What do we need him for?"

"Shhh," said Friday. "Listen."

"Miss Priddock," began Mr. Maclean, "are those chocolate cookies I spy on your desk? Would you like me to relieve you of the temptation of eating one by eating it myself?"

Miss Priddock giggled.

They heard Mr. Maclean's footsteps, then the sound of him using his key to open his pigeonhole. "Miss

Priddock, I love the blouse you're wearing," said Mr. Maclean. "Sienna brings out the highlights in your hair. It's like a breath of sunshine."

"I think I'm going to be sick," said Simmons.

"I know," said Friday. "Breath of sunshine. It's an absurd mixed metaphor. You have a breath of fresh air. Or a ray of sunshine."

"Is that what this is all about, then?" asked the Headmaster. "You're making a complaint about Mr. Maclean flirting with Miss Priddock?"

"Indirectly, yes," agreed Friday. "Although we don't have a problem in principle with Mr. Maclean making a fool of himself in front of the younger members of the school's secretarial staff."

Mr. Maclean stuck his head around the Headmaster's door. "I got a message you wanted to see me, Headmaster," he said.

"Not I," said the Headmaster. "No, you have been summoned here because you have somehow transgressed in the eyes of the great Friday Barnes."

Mr. Maclean looked at the small, dull-looking girl before him. His brain was struggling to understand what was going on. "Oh, Balmes. Yes, what's the problem?"

"Mr. Maclean, we are here today because you wrongly accused Simmons of handing in his assignment two days late," stated Friday.

"What?" said Mr. Maclean. He was unused to being challenged. When you practiced smiling as much as he did it just didn't happen very often. "Don't be ridiculous. I check my pigeonhole every day. And I mark the date on the papers as soon as I get to my desk."

"Hmm," said Friday, "I shall accept that statement. I have no reason to disbelieve it."

"Then what on earth are you talking about?" said Mr. Maclean.

"If we all adjourn to the pigeonholes, I shall show you," said Friday.

"Do we have to?" asked Mr. Maclean.

"Yes, you do have to," said the Headmaster. He was enjoying seeing Mr. Maclean being discomforted. He resented the fact that Mr. Maclean had greater access to chocolate cookies just because he was good-looking.

They all trudged out into the lobby and over to the pigeonholes, except for Simmons, who of course limped.

"This is a ridiculous waste of time," grumbled Mr. Maclean.

"I can assure you that as a geography teacher your time isn't really that valuable," Friday pointed out. "If we had to monetize it using salary data and quality-of-life estimates, I would say the three minutes this interaction has taken us so far would, at best, be worth about two dollars and thirty cents."

"Can we move it along please, Friday?" said the Headmaster. "I imagine that crime fighting is enormously amusing for you, but you really should try to attend some of your classes during the course of the day."

"Of course," said Friday. "Now, Mr. Maclean, you just emptied your pigeonhole, didn't you? This pigeonhole at the end in the top row? And before you answer, I should inform you that we know the answer is yes because we heard you do it."

"Well then, yes, I just emptied my pigeonhole," said Mr. Maclean.

"And what did you find in your pigeonhole?" asked Friday.

"I haven't had a chance to look yet," said Mr. Maclean.

"Look now," said Friday.

Mr. Maclean looked at the stack of papers in his hand. "These are eighth-grade assignments."

"Is that all there is in that stack?" asked Friday.

"I think so," said Mr. Maclean.

"Check," said Friday.

"This is preposterous," said Mr. Maclean.

"Yes, yes," said the Headmaster. "Just do it."

Mr. Maclean leafed through the assignments. "It's just assignments," he said. "Hang on, wait a minute. At the bottom there is something else." Mr. Maclean took out the bottom sheet of paper from the stack. There was something typed in the middle of the page. Mr. Maclean balked.

"What does it say?" asked Friday.

"It says, 'You missed something,'" said Mr. Maclean.

"How interesting," said Friday. "Now, if you would be so kind as to open your pigeonhole, we can see just what you missed."

Now even Mr. Maclean was curious. He took out his key and opened the door. The pigeonhole was above his eye line, so none of them could see anything inside.

"Put your hand in and feel around," said Friday.

Mr. Maclean reached in. "There's nothing . . . Hang

on, there is something." He reached in a little farther and pulled out some more paper.

"What do those sheets say?" asked Friday.

"You missed me, and me, and me," said Mr. Maclean, reading off the pages. "What is the meaning of this? I've been set up. You put these in my pigeonhole."

"Yes I did," agreed Friday. "To prove a point. When you empty your pigeonhole you always turn and flirt with Miss Priddock, the receptionist, as you do it."

"I do no such thing," protested Mr. Maclean.

"Ahem," said the Headmaster. "I heard you doing it myself, just this morning."

"Well, I like to make friendly chitchat with the support staff; it's good for morale," said Mr. Maclean.

"Yes, well, luckily, we are not here to discuss your dubious behavioral standards," said Friday. "I am merely trying to establish that you don't pay attention to what you are doing when you empty your pigeonhole. The pigeonhole is quite high, and you can't see into it easily. So if a paper became partially stuck to the bottom, you probably wouldn't notice."

"But why would a paper become stuck to my pigeonhole?" exclaimed Mr. Maclean. "It's ridiculous."

"You really need to consult a thesaurus," said Friday, shaking her head. "Your vocabulary lacks variety and precision. Your pigeonhole would become sticky if someone left something sticky in there. Allow me . . ."

Friday stepped toward the pigeonhole. She had to stand up on her tiptoes, but she reached in and scraped the bottom of the pigeonhole with her finger. She looked at her finger, then sniffed it.

"Gross!" said Simmons.

Friday then dabbed her finger against the taste buds on her tongue as she concentrated. "Confectioner's sugar, lemon zest, and custard. Tell me, has anyone given you a lemon tart recently?"

Mr. Maclean blushed. "No."

"Hmm," said Friday. "Perhaps I should have phrased that differently. Have you been in possession of a lemon tart recently?"

Mr. Maclean looked shifty. "Maybe," he conceded.

"Did you perhaps steal one from Miss Priddock's desk?" asked Friday.

"No!" exclaimed Mr. Maclean. "Don't be ridiculous. Of course not."

"Let's examine the facts," said Friday. "There was a

lemon tart in your pigeonhole. And a lemon tart went missing from Miss Priddock's desk. I believe you took it when Miss Priddock was away from her desk. You reasoned that she would have given it to you if she was there, so it was all the same. And yet you had a guilty conscience because when Miss Priddock entered, you quickly dropped the illicit lemon tart through the slip in your pigeonhole to hide the evidence, waiting until you would be able to hide it better by eating it secretly in the privacy of the office."

"This is ridiculous," spluttered Mr. Maclean.

"Five times," said Melanie.

"Five what?" asked the Headmaster.

"He's said 'ridiculous' five times," explained Melanie.

"You make it sound like a criminal conspiracy," said Mr. Maclean. "It was just a lemon tart."

"A lemon tart that fell facedown in your pigeonhole, causing lemon custard to smear on the bottom, which adhered to Simmons's assignment. It did not slide out with your other paperwork; it sat glued to the bottom for an extra two days. At that time you docked his marks and he was expelled from the lacrosse team," said Friday. "I call that a lemon tart with serious consequences."

"Well, Maclean," said the Headmaster, "it sounds like you've got two marks to adjust. You need to correct Simmons's grade for the unjust time penalty, and you'd better buy a new packet of lemon tarts for Miss Priddock, in the interests of staff morale, specifically mine."

Simmons leaped in the air. "Hurray, I can play lacrosse again!" Then he collapsed on the ground because, of course, his knees hurt.

"I have one more question for Mr. Maclean," said Friday.

The Headmaster sighed. "Friday, you've won your argument. You really need to learn to quit while you're ahead."

"It is in relation to another matter," said Friday. "I'd like to know what Mr. Maclean was doing yesterday in the swamp. You weren't impersonating a yeti, were you? We know you like to impress people. And what better way to impress people than to dress up like a wild beast and scare the daylights out of them, particularly Miss Harrow, who is very attractive and probably not easily impressed by a practiced smile?"

Mr. Maclean looked confounded for a moment, then burst out laughing. "Balmes," he said between chuckles, "perhaps your IQ test was a statistical error after all. As if I'd ever dress up as an ape-man! I'm a geography teacher. I was in the swamp preparing a lesson on the ecosystem of the wetlands." Mr. Maclean smiled one of his practiced smiles.

"He's lying," said Melanie.

"Melanie Pelly," snapped the Headmaster, "accusing a member of the teaching staff of lying is a very serious matter indeed."

"Oh, I wasn't accusing him," said Melanie. "I was just letting Friday know. She's brilliant with facts but not so strong on social nuance."

"I am not lying," said Mr. Maclean.

"Okay," said Melanie, who turned and looked at Friday while raising her eyebrows meaningfully.

"It's okay, Melanie," said Friday. "Even I can interpret that one."

Two days later, Friday was sitting in the dining hall eating breakfast when the bursar brought over a large package for her.

"Who sent that?" asked Melanie.

"It's from my uncle Bernie," said Friday. "It must be the clothes I asked for."

Friday tore open the package. There were three pairs of jeans, several black T-shirts, and two brown cardigans. Friday picked up a cardigan and pressed the soft acrylic-wool blend to her cheek.

"Wasn't he going to get you something nice?" asked Melanie.

"I asked him to," said Friday with a smile, "but Uncle Bernie likes me just the way I am."

At the bottom of the package was a separate box. This wasn't wrapped in brown packing paper like the rest of the clothes. It was gift-wrapped properly with shiny red paper. Friday tore this open a little more carefully. Inside was a hatbox. There was a handwritten note from Uncle Bernie sticky-taped to the lid.

Dear Friday,
It is traditional for all great detectives to wear a silly hat, so I thought you would be needing this.
                              Love,
                              Uncle Bernie

Friday opened the box. Inside was a green felt pork-pie hat. Friday lifted it out with care. She smiled, then put her new detective hat on her head. It fell down to her eyebrows. It was too large.

"People are going to think you are eccentric if you wear that," said Melanie.

"And they will be one hundred percent correct," said Friday. She grinned at Melanie. "I love it."

# The Case of the Missing Homework

Barnes . . . Barnes!"

Friday was sitting in the dining hall, eating dinner. It was Wednesday and the meal was pot roast, which was the second-best dinner of the week, so Friday did not enjoy having it interrupted.

She turned to see Parker, a ninth-grade boy, running toward her.

"You've got to help me!" he cried as he came to a panting halt beside her.

"I've got to, have I?" said Friday.

"You should have said 'please,' " said Melanie.

"Please, Barnes," said Parker. "I'm in big trouble."

"My first name is Friday," said Friday. "I know you boys insist on referring to each other by your surnames, but I'm not a boy, so I don't like it."

"Sorry, Friday," said Parker. "You will help me, won't you? I'll pay you. Here . . ." He rummaged in his pockets and found a twenty-dollar bill. "I've got a twenty right here if you just come and have a look. And I'll give you another twenty if you can find it."

"Find what?" asked Friday. Her irritation with Parker could not dampen her natural curiosity for a mystery.

"My assignment. It's worth 80 percent of my final grade for the year," said Parker. "And someone stole it. I think it was"—he leaned in close—"the swamp yeti."

"Intriguing," said Friday.

"Why would the swamp yeti want your assignment?" asked Melanie.

"I heard a rumor that the swamp yeti was a student from long ago who ran away from being in seventh grade," said Parker. "So perhaps he's tired of living in the swamp with all the mosquitoes and stinky mud, and he's trying to catch up on the coursework so he can get back in."

"We shall investigate," announced Friday.

Friday and Melanie went with Parker back to his room. It was just like their own, except that it smelled bad because two boys lived there, and there was lots of dirty sports equipment littered about. (Friday and Melanie did not approve of sports equipment. If they were forced to own any, they usually shoved it as far back underneath their beds as possible so they would never have to look at it.)

"Talk me through what happened," said Friday.

"I was sitting here doing my chemistry assignment," said Parker. "It was really hard. It took me forever. I'm not very good at understanding valences. I know the teacher said it had something to do with an orange and a baseball field, but, honestly, I couldn't follow what the fellow was saying."

"So it took you a while?" asked Friday.

"Hours and hours," replied Parker. "My roommate, Nigel, had to go and get me a plate of dinner so I could work right through."

"It was shepherd's pie last night," said Melanie.

"You wouldn't want to miss that. It's the best dinner of the week."

"Absolutely," agreed Parker. "But I couldn't afford time away from my desk. The assignment's due tomorrow and I just had to get it done."

"Couldn't you ask for an extension?" asked Friday.

"Normally I would," replied Parker. "But Mr. Spencer would never do that. He hates me."

"Why?" asked Friday. "It seems very unscientific to be so emotional."

"Because in the last exam when we had to identify which beaker contained acid and which contained an alkaline, I forgot how to do the proper tests with that litmus stuff, so I worked it out by sticking my finger in each beaker and licking it."

"Oh, I remember that," said Melanie. "You had to spend a week in the hospital, didn't you?"

"That's right," said Parker. "It was an awesome week. I got to lie in bed all day watching television. And the skin grew back eventually, so all in all it was a win for me."

Friday peered at Parker's desk, and then the window next to it. "How was it that your homework came to be missing?" asked Friday.

"I was struggling with a particularly difficult problem and eating the first bite of my shepherd's pie when Portelli knocked on the door," explained Parker. "He said they'd tied a sixth-grade boy to a desk leg, and did I want to go and have a look."

"And you did?" asked Friday.

"Of course," said Parker. "It sounded like a laugh. So I popped out for a quick peek. I was only gone sixty seconds, and when I came back it was gone!"

"Someone had taken your homework?" asked Friday.

"Yes, and to add insult to injury they took my dinner as well," said Parker.

"They ate your dinner?" asked Friday.

"Yes," said Parker.

"Did they take the plate?" asked Friday.

"What difference does that make?" asked Parker.

"I'm not sure yet," said Friday. She was clearly lost in concentration.

"No, they left the plate, but ate every last scrap of the dinner," said Parker. "It's a good thing I had a stash of potato chips hidden under the floorboards, or I would have starved."

Friday looked about the room, then walked over to the open window, took out a magnifying glass, and closely inspected the frame.

"Hmm," she said.

"A clue?" asked Parker.

"A footprint," said Friday.

"Whose is it?" asked Parker. "It's the swamp yeti, isn't it?"

"No," said Friday. "Swamp yetis don't exist."

"Oh," said Parker. He was clearly disappointed.

Friday leaned out the window, looking first one way,

then the other. On one side she could see the baseball field in the distance. On the other side she could see boys coming out of the dining hall, laughing among themselves and throwing a few scraps to Fudge, the school's overweight dog.

"Then do you know who did take my homework?" asked Parker.

"Yes, I do," said Friday. "The problem will be proving it. I've got the twenty you just gave me, but do you have any more cash?"

"Umm," said Parker as he checked his pockets. "I've got eighty . . . no, ninety dollars."

"That ought to do it," said Friday, taking the money out of his hand. "What time is your science lesson tomorrow?"

"Third period," said Parker. "So 11:15 a.m."

"I can make that work," said Friday as she tucked the cash in her pocket. "I will meet you at the beginning of your science class tomorrow with your stolen homework."

Friday then turned and clambered out the window.

"Thank you, thank you very much!" Parker called after her with great relief.

He and Melanie watched Friday jog off into the bushes. Parker turned to Melanie. "She hasn't just run off with my money, has she?"

"I don't think so," said Melanie. "But it can be hard to tell with Friday sometimes. She's very peculiar."

# Chapter
## 18
# The Homework Is Found

The next morning Parker was very nervous as he stood outside his science classroom, waiting for Friday. Melanie waited with him. But that did not make him less nervous because Parker found girls nerve-racking as well. All the other students were filing in. He couldn't delay much longer.

Mr. Spencer was just about to start the lesson when he spotted his hapless student loitering in the corridor.

"Parker, get in here, stop dillydallying," he snapped.

Parker entered. His shoulders were slumped. He was just about to get detention for goodness knows how many days, possibly weeks. And he was out of pocket the $110 he had already given Friday.

"Why is *she* here?" asked Mr. Spencer as he glared at Melanie. She had followed Parker into the room. "Did you decide to bring a date to class?"

The class sniggered.

"No, sir," said Parker lamely.

"And where's your assignment?" continued Mr. Spencer.

"I don't have it, sir," said Parker.

Mr. Spencer sighed and crossed his arms, getting ready to enjoy yelling at his most abysmal student. "So, tell me, what's your excuse this time?"

"Someone stole it," said Parker.

"Preposterous!" exclaimed Mr. Spencer. "You expect me to believe that someone would steal the homework of a boy like you?"

"It sounds silly when you put it that way," agreed Parker.

Suddenly the door burst open.

"Stop!" yelled Friday as she stood in the entrance, carrying a ziplock bag containing a mysterious brown substance.

"What are you doing here?" demanded Mr. Spencer. "Aren't you in seventh grade? Shouldn't you be in English right now?"

"A minor technicality," said Friday. "I am here to clear the name of this boy, Parker."

"He says someone stole his homework," said Mr. Spencer. "I find that very hard to believe. When he does hand in assignments he always gets very bad grades. No one in his right mind would steal an assignment from him."

"Ah," said Friday, "but it wasn't stolen. It was eaten!"

"What?!" exclaimed Parker and Mr. Spencer in unison.

"By whom?" asked Mr. Spencer.

"Not 'By whom?'" said Friday. "The question you should ask is 'By what?'"

"So it *was* the swamp yeti!" exclaimed Parker.

"No," said Friday. "Your homework was not eaten by another student or a fictional swamp-dwelling man-beast. It was eaten by Fudge, the school dog."

"Fudge ate my homework?" marveled Parker. "But why would he do that? He always gets lots of scraps from the students. That's why he's so fat."

"Because it was shepherd's pie Tuesday," said Friday, "and everyone loves Mrs. Marigold's shepherd's pie. Therefore, there were no scraps. It is the one day of the week when Fudge is left alone outside the dining room windows, feeling hungry. And there is nothing hungrier than a fat dog. So when you left your plate of shepherd's pie on your desk it was practically entrapment. Fudge could not resist."

"But what has that got to do with this boy's homework?" asked Mr. Spencer.

"Dogs are messy eaters," explained Friday. "They usually eat from bowls. But Parker's shepherd's pie was on a plate. So as Fudge licked it up, he licked it off the plate and onto the piece of paper below, which was the homework assignment. When he finished, Fudge was still hungry, so he ate the gravy-smeared paper as well. Dogs don't have opposable thumbs, so they literally can't pick and choose what they eat."

"This is absurd," said Mr. Spencer. "I don't believe it for a minute."

"Ah, but I have proof!" said Friday as she held up the ziplock bag full of mysterious brown stuff. Everyone in the room got a nasty suspicion about just what was in that bag. "Behold! Here is Parker's assignment. Fully digested and excreted as Fudge's poop!"

"Ewww!" exclaimed the students.

"That's disgusting!" exclaimed Mr. Spencer.

"That's evidence," said Friday. "I had an express courier drive it to the university last night. There is a PhD student there who owes me a favor because I helped him with the mathematics in his thesis. He ran a sample of the poop through their analysis protocols, and the results are conclusive. This poop is eleven percent paper, which is consistent with a sheet of letter-size paper eaten along with a serving of shepherd's pie."

"This is by far the most disgusting thing a student has ever confronted me with," said Mr. Spencer.

"Disgusting, yes, but also conclusive proof that a dog ate Parker's homework," said Friday.

The class applauded. Friday was putting on their most interesting science lesson since Mr. Spencer accidentally burned his own eyebrows off with a Bunsen burner.

"This whole debacle still does not reflect well on Parker. I have a good mind to send him to detention anyway," said Mr. Spencer.

"Mr. Spencer," said Friday, "I know that Parker is as thick as two short planks, and that must be very irritating for you to endure. But he is sincerely frightened of you, and so he did earnestly try to do his assignment. If you crush him now, it may be a blow he never recovers from. And you don't want Parker to repeat a year because his grades are so bad, do you?"

"No," said Mr. Spencer, shuddering at the thought of having to endure another twelve months with the dullard.

"So give him another night to do the assignment all over again," suggested Friday.

"Aww," said Parker, "I was hoping I could get a pass."

"Parker," said Mr. Spencer, "I'm giving you another chance. But please don't leave a freshly cooked meal on top of your homework in front of an open window again."

"No danger of that, sir," said Parker. "It's kidney pie for dinner tonight. Not even Fudge would touch that."

"Well done," said Melanie as the two girls left Mr. Spencer's classroom.

"It was simple, really," said Friday. "The only hard part was following Fudge around until he pooped. I didn't realize that the canine digestive system was so slow."

"It's just a shame it was Fudge," said Melanie.

"What do you mean?" asked Friday.

"Well, it's one thing to have a yeti living in the swamp," said Melanie, "but to have him climbing in through windows looking for food would be even more exciting."

"Setting aside the fact that swamp yetis do not exist," said Friday, "what on earth would be exciting about having one climb in through your window?"

Melanie sighed. "Friday, you need to read fewer textbooks and more romance novels—then you'd know.

Speaking of which, do you know where Ian has been this week?"

"No," said Friday.

"If he doesn't turn up soon," said Melanie, "you should make him the subject of your next investigation."

"Why would I do that?" asked Friday.

"Because of your feelings for him, of course," said Melanie.

"If he had disappeared into the swamp and been eaten by the swamp yeti, that would be fine with me," said Friday.

"Ahuh," said Melanie, who did not want to accuse her best friend of being a liar.

# 19

# The Case of
the A++

Ian did turn up several days later, but not in the dramatic style Friday had been expecting. When Friday and Melanie entered Mr. Braithwaite's history class, Ian Wainscott was setting up to do a presentation at the front of the room. He was looking like his usual detached and aloof self, except browner. He had an incredibly good tan. When Friday had last seen him, Ian had the usual pale skin of a blond boy in winter, but now he was practically

copper-colored, except for a watch mark on his left wrist, which clearly showed what color his skin had been when they'd last seen him a week earlier.

"I didn't know Ian was back," said Friday.

"Oh yes," said Melanie. "I saw a car pull up and drop him off after breakfast. I didn't like to mention it to you because I know how you are in love with him, and I thought it would affect your ability to concentrate during class."

"I'm not in love with Ian Wainscott," hissed Friday.

"Oh no," agreed Melanie. "Of course you're not." She nodded amiably, clearly not believing Friday for a second.

Friday sighed. There was no point arguing with Melanie. Words had very little semiotic meaning for her. She usually lost concentration somewhere between the beginning and the end of a sentence.

"I wonder if he will beat you," said Melanie. "It looks like he's got lots of props."

All the students in the class had had to present a fifteen-minute talk on a historical subject of their choice. Friday had received an A+ for her presentation on Rosalind Franklin and how Watson, Crick, and ovarian cancer had combined to cheat her out of a Nobel Prize for her role in the discovery of the struc-ture of DNA. That A+ was the top grade in the class so far. Ian was the last to do his presentation because he'd been away.

"History presentations are not a competitive sport," said Friday snappily.

"They should be," said Melanie. "Making assign-ments competitive makes much more sense than mak-ing sports competitive. That's just kicking a ball around. Who cares about that?"

"Okay, Ian," said Mr. Braithwaite. "When you're ready."

The mumble among the students fell silent. Ian really was very handsome. When you actually looked at him, and he looked at you with those piercing blue eyes, it was hard to remember what you were think-ing about in the first place.

"Some of you are probably wondering where I was last week," said Ian.

Actually, few of the students were. People often un-derestimate how self-involved everyone is. As the say-ing goes, "You would not worry so much what others think of you if you realized how rarely they did."

"I was in Egypt," announced Ian.

This set the class off muttering again.

"Shhh," said Mr. Braithwaite, who resented having to pay attention to class control during a presentation. He usually saw it as an opportunity to have a rest.

"I was helping with an archaeological dig," said Ian. "My cousin is in charge of the excavation of Abu Simbel, the site of the statue of Ramses the Great."

Ian took out a large color photograph of a huge stone statue of a king.

The class gasped. The Egyptians were undeniably impressive when it came to public monuments.

"You can see me standing in the foreground," said Ian.

The class leaned in. On closer

inspection they could see Ian. They hadn't realized he was in the photo because they hadn't realized just how huge the statue of Ramses the Great was. Ian seemed like an insect in the foreground.

"It was hard, dusty work," said Ian. "I spent five days brushing away sand with a soft paintbrush without finding anything. But on the sixth day I found this."

Ian showed a photograph of himself crouching in an archaeological dig. He had the soft brush in his right hand, and in his other hand he held up a coin. It was clearly a very old coin. He had taken off his glove. It was the same dark brown as his leather watch strap. He held the coin up at eye level, just next to the scar above his eye.

"It is a coin from the time when the Romans

controlled Egypt," explained Ian. "You can see it has a picture of Julius Caesar on it. And here it is." Ian took the coin out of his pocket and passed it around. "I was allowed to bring it home to show you."

"Looks like you're going to lose, Barnes," Mirabella obnoxiously called out from the front of the class. "Ian's topped your tedious speech. He's sure to get an A++."

"He deserves an A++," said Friday.

"Thank you," said Ian, smirking at her.

"If he is being given marks for lying badly," continued Friday. "But for history he should get an F because he's made three critical mistakes."

"He has?" said Mr. Braithwaite, snapping out of his reverie. He had been imagining what he would make for dinner. He was thinking of trying to make horseradish sauce from scratch.

"First of all," said Friday, "Ian can't have worked on a dig at the site of the statue of Ramses the Great because that whole area was flooded by the construction of the Aswan Dam."

Ian turned red.

"The statues were moved," continued Friday. "They

are not in their original location. To explore the original location would require scuba gear."

"I can scuba dive," argued Ian.

"I'm sure you can," said Friday. "But do you have access to a time machine? You'd need one if what you said is true, because Julius Caesar was long dead when Rome took control of Egypt. It was Octavius Caesar who commanded the Roman forces at that time. Anyone who has ever seen the play *Antony and Cleopatra* could tell you that."

"Old Roman currency must have still been in circulation," protested Ian.

"Fair enough," said Friday. "But you made one more crucial error." She got up from her desk and walked over to confront Ian.

"What are you talking about?" asked Ian guardedly.

"This," said Friday. She licked her thumb and ran it down the side of Ian's face.

"Ewww," chorused the class.

Ian flinched.

Friday turned around and showed the class her thumb. It was as brown as leather.

"He is wearing fake tan," said Friday. "A very good fake tan, except for one small detail. In the photo you're wearing your watch on your left wrist, and holding the coin up to the left side of your face, next to your eye with the scar above it. But here you are in real life, with the watch tan line on your left wrist. But your scar is, and always has been, over your right eye. You faked the photographs digitally, then put on a fake tan to lend credibility to your story. But you forgot to allow for the mirroring of the image."

Everyone in the class glanced from the photo to Ian and back several times. Friday was clearly correct.

"She's right," concluded Mr. Braithwaite.

"I hate you," seethed Ian. He threw the coin at Friday and stormed out of the room.

The whole class erupted into frenzied speculation.

Except for Friday. She was contemplative as she picked up the old coin.

"Oh dear," said Melanie. "You've embarrassed him. This is going to drive an even bigger wedge in your relationship."

"There is more to this than meets the eye," said Friday.

"He was cheating on a history assignment," said

Melanie. "We've all done that. Or, well, I would have if I'd had the energy."

"But he did it so badly, with such slipshod research," said Friday. "That's not like Ian. He's very bright. He enjoys being devious. He normally takes delight in getting all the little details right. This charade was a rush job. His mind is on other things. And where was he last week? He clearly wasn't on an archaeological dig in Egypt. This whole debacle is curious indeed."

# Chapter
# 20
# Something Spooky

Several days later, Friday and Melanie were fast asleep in bed. Well, Friday's conscious was asleep while her unconscious was being coached in Russian. Friday found if she listened to language tapes as she slept, after a few months her brain would teach itself to be bilingual (actually, multilingual—she had forced several languages into her brain over the years). Anyway, it was the middle of

the night when their sleep was interrupted by a duo of high-pitched screaming.

"Waaaaaagggghhhhh!" screamed the voices.

Friday immediately leaped out of bed. "What was that?"

"Was it me?" asked Melanie. "Sometimes I wake up screaming when I remember that I have a math assignment due."

"No, it was definitely someone downstairs," said Friday as she hurriedly put on her dressing gown. "Come on, let's see what it was."

The girls went out into the corridor and discovered a couple of dozen equally curious students investigating the noise. Down in the lobby were two panting seventh-grade boys who looked like they'd had the living daylights scared out of them.

"Let's interrogate them," said Friday.

Friday and Melanie were making their way through the crowd when Mr. Franklin, the dormitory supervisor, burst into the lobby. Everyone sniggered. Mr. Franklin was usually a model of propriety, so to see him in his dressing gown and slippers, no matter how respectable the dressing gown and slippers were, was comical.

"What is the meaning of this?" demanded Mr. Franklin. "What are you two boys doing out of bed and screaming at this ridiculous hour?"

"We were in the swamp!" said Benny.

"And we saw the beast!" exclaimed Fred.

No one laughed, even though it was a bizarre statement. Fred said it with such sincerity everyone could tell he wasn't joking.

"Don't be farcical," said Mr. Franklin. "There's no such thing as the beast."

"But we saw one," declared Benny. "It growled at us. It had huge teeth, hair everywhere. It was awful."

"An awful cliché," muttered Friday.

"You didn't see it," said Fred defensively. "If you did, you'd be screaming, too."

"What were you doing at the swamp anyway?" asked Mr. Franklin. "You know if a classmate throws your belongings in the swamp, you are meant to report it to the school secretary and she will arrange for a member of the maintenance staff to fetch it for you."

"We were buying a phone," said Fred.

"But phones aren't allowed," said Melanie.

"That's why we were buying it in the middle of the night," said Benny.

"This is ridiculous fiddle-faddle," said Mr. Franklin as he moved toward the front door. "Both of you report to the Headmaster's office at eight tomorrow morning. Right now, all of you should go to bed." Mr. Franklin reached out to lock the door, but he was knocked backward when Ian Wainscott stumbled in, panting. He slammed the door and locked it himself. His face was as white as a sheet.

"What were you doing outside at this hour?" demanded Mr. Franklin.

"He was the one who was going to sell us the phone," said Fred.

"Thanks for your discretion, boys," Ian said sarcastically. "I categorically deny it all. I was outside because I heard two young boys screaming and I was concerned."

"Huh, a likely story," said Friday.

"All right, you can see the Headmaster in the morning, too. Now everyone get to bed," said Mr. Franklin.

No one moved. They were all burning with curiosity. And the boys who had been outside clearly wanted to tell everybody about it.

"Off to bed, or I shall leave the door wide open

and let the wild hairy ape-man in," threatened Mr. Franklin.

All the children scuttled back to their rooms.

"You don't think there really is a wild ape-man in the swamp?" asked Melanie as she lay in bed with the blankets tucked up to her chin.

Friday was sitting up in bed, sucking a lollipop, as her brain whizzed like a computer hard drive processing all the various possibilities. "No," said Friday, "because they don't exist. But it is very intriguing. So many variables, so many possibilities."

"I suppose we'd better go back to sleep," said Melanie.

"Oh, there's no chance of that," said Friday. "This is all way too fascinating. I'll sleep tomorrow in math instead."

# Chapter

## 21

# The Plot Thickens

Friday did not get a chance to quiz Benny or Fred the next day. They weren't at breakfast, and by the end of first period, word had spread around the school that they had both been suspended for a week for being on the grounds after lights-out. Also, Benny's father wanted to send him to Switzerland for therapy because he claimed he was suffering post-traumatic stress disorder, which could only be cured by a week of skiing.

The only witness to the

ape-man's attack who remained was Ian Wainscott. He'd been let off because his story was so convincing. Good-looking people are so much more convincing when they lie.

Friday had developed a healthy dislike for Ian based on the enormous dislike he clearly showed for her. But her curiosity overcame her natural sense of self-preservation (not her greatest instinct at the best of times) when she saw him on her way to history class.

"Ian," called Friday as she stepped out of the flow of foot traffic.

Ian turned and sneered at her. "What do you want?"

Friday ignored the unpleasantries. "I want to ask you a few questions."

"What a surprise," said Ian. "The girl detective wants to stick her nose in where it doesn't belong."

"What happened last night?" asked Friday, again ignoring his provocation.

Ian leaned forward so that he was right in Friday's face, then said with barely controlled anger, "None of your business." He turned and walked away.

"Were you playing pranks again?" Friday called after him.

Ian just ignored her. Friday watched him go.

"You're falling even more in love with him, aren't you?" said Melanie.

"What?" said Friday.

"When people bicker like that in movies, it's always because they are secretly in love with each other and they're trying to fight it," said Melanie.

"I'm not secretly in love with Ian Wainscott," said Friday.

"Okay," said Melanie. "But the people in movies never realize they are secretly in love either."

"What are you talking about?" asked Friday. She was barely paying attention because her mind was preoccupied with beasts, swamps, and what Ian could possibly be up to.

"Come on," said Melanie. "We'd better hurry up or we'll be really late for biology. And I don't want to be sent to the Headmaster's office, because on Tuesday, Miss Harrow always has new birds in her aviary."

"You're birdbrained," said Friday grumpily.

"My mother often tells me the same thing," said Melanie. "But if I had a brain the size of a grain of rice and I could fly, I think I'd be happy with that."

The girls trudged off to class.

# More Screaming

That night the girls went to sleep as usual. Melanie dreamed about being a bird or a butterfly or some other pretty thing that flitted about. Friday lay in a semidormant state, her half-conscious brain processing all the information it had input during the course of the day. Beasts in swamps and frighteningly good-looking boys with anger management issues were so much more interesting than coursework. And apparently

several schoolgirls agreed with Friday's sentiments entirely, because at 2:17 a.m. exactly the entire school was again awoken by screaming.

"There's someone screaming in the hall again," said Friday.

"Maybe they can't decide what to wear tomorrow," said Melanie sleepily.

"Come on, let's investigate," said Friday. "I can make out five voices this time. And they sound like girls." Friday was hurrying to put her slippers and robe on.

"The boys yesterday sounded like girls when they were screaming," said Melanie.

"Yes," agreed Friday. "Their pitch was just as high. But when girls scream like that it sounds different. It goes on and on. You can tell they are enjoying themselves."

Friday and Melanie bustled down to the entrance lobby, and Friday was proved correct. A crowd had gathered around five hysterical girls who were clearly having a wonderful time being scared out of their wits (not that they had a lot of wits to start with) because they could barely keep the grins off their faces.

Mr. Franklin burst out of his room. "What is the

meaning of this?!" This time he was wearing a track-suit. He'd had the good sense to go to bed wearing outdoor clothes after the embarrassment of letting half the student body see his pajamas the night before.

"We saw the swamp yeti!" announced Trea breathlessly.

Observing Trea's wide eyes and gushing tone, Friday reflected that in days gone by she would have been slapped in the face for hysteria.

"What were you doing out on the grounds?" demanded Mr. Franklin.

"Looking for the man-beast," admitted another girl, and then they all giggled. Whatever genuine fear they'd suffered had now ebbed away in the security of the dormitory building, and the whole experience was now just good fun.

"Why on earth would you go out into the swamp in the middle of the night, looking for a wild beast?" asked Mr. Franklin. Being a sixty-year-old man, the complexities of a teenage girl's mind were beyond him.

"Because rugged, untamed men are cute," said Trea. Now lots of girls giggled.

"There is a subsection of literature that depicts teenage werewolves and foundlings raised by apes as objects of romantic aspiration," Friday told Mr. Franklin helpfully.

Mr. Franklin glared at Friday, then the other girls. He had thought he'd seen it all as a teacher. But every year the children seemed to become sillier in ways that he never could have imagined.

"All of you, go to bed," snapped Mr. Franklin. "You five," he said to Trea and her four friends, "and you"— he pointed at Friday—"report to the Headmaster's office at eight tomorrow morning."

"What did I do?" protested Friday.

"You're too clever for your own good," said Mr. Franklin.

"Scholarship girl," said Trea spitefully as they all turned and went to bed, already mentally planning the splendid week Friday would have at home while under suspension.

# 23

# Back in the Headmaster's Office

The next morning Friday and the other five girls were sitting on the bench outside the Headmaster's office. The Headmaster kept them waiting. Friday wondered if he was hiding around the corner and peeking to see if they would stay sitting there. He eventually

appeared, bustling along the corridor and looking grumpy as usual.

"You again," he said to Friday as he walked past on the way to his office. He pushed the door open and turned to the gigglers. "You five, come in," he said sternly, which of course made them giggle. "You, wait," he said, glaring at Friday. Friday was delighted to oblige. Sitting outside the Headmaster's office was getting her out of woodwork. And as she had already taught herself fine woodworking skills from watching You-Tube clips, she didn't feel that learning how to make a bookend would teach her very much.

Friday listened to the Headmaster telling the other girls off. She couldn't hear the words he was using because the school had thick walls, but she could hear his tone. It was a low, rumbling monotone. *He's trying to bore them to death,* suspected Friday. But the monotone gradually grew louder and louder until the Headmaster started shouting. The shouting came in staccato bursts. Friday could catch the occasional word: words like "ashamed" and "disappointed" as well as adjectives like "abysmal," "irresponsible," and "pathetic." He wound it up with a few hard thumps on the desk. She heard footsteps across the floor, and then the door swung open and Friday could see the Headmaster standing angrily in the doorway of his office as the five girls, now totally deflated, emerged sobbing and red-eyed. They were so consumed by their own self-pity that they didn't even look at Friday as they walked past.

"You, in here," ordered the Headmaster, pointing his finger at Friday. Friday felt uncharacteristic discomfort and trepidation. The Headmaster clearly had his blood up. He was on a roll with doling out punishment.

She walked quietly into his office. There was a chair in front of his desk, but she knew it was a trick and she should not sit in it unless invited to.

The Headmaster walked behind his desk and stood next to his chair. He glared at Friday, then sat down. "What do you have to say for yourself?"

"Nothing," said Friday.

"Really?" said the Headmaster. "How uncharacteristic. I thought you had an opinion on every topic. Mr. Franklin claims you were making wisecracks last night."

"I think he misunderstood me," said Friday. "It was

late. I was only trying to be helpful and provide a factual background."

"You are too helpful for your own good," said the Headmaster darkly.

Friday frowned. She felt this was a profoundly flawed and illogical statement. But using what was for her a rare flash of insight into human nature, she judged that now was not the time to point that out.

Friday looked at the Headmaster and he glared back at her.

"So tell me, since you're the smarty-pants, what is going on down at the swamp?" asked the Headmaster.

"I don't know!" said Friday. She was surprised by the question.

"Really? I thought you had the answers to everything," said the Headmaster.

"No," admitted Friday. "It only seems that way because I do know a lot more than the average eleven-year-old. I know a lot more than most adults as well."

The Headmaster sighed. "But apparently you don't know when to keep quiet."

"I think I have been thrown off balance by the sub-culture of this school," said Friday. "I was very good at being quiet before. I could go weeks without talking to anyone. But here, people keep asking me provocative rhetorical questions. And I've never been very good at picking up on when a question is rhetorical. I know it's something you're supposed to be able to gauge from watching facial expressions and listening to voice tone, but that is something I have not been able to teach myself from a book."

The Headmaster sighed again and rubbed his head. He didn't actually have a headache yet, but it was only quarter past eight in the morning and he was sure he would have one by the end of the day.

"I have suspended seven students in two days," said the Headmaster. "There are only 278 students in the school. At this rate there will be none left by the end of the month."

"Actually, if you graphed the trend and it continued on the same arc," said Friday, "we'd all be gone in four days. Because you suspended five students today and two yesterday. Five is two times two and a half. Five times two and a half is twelve and a half, but we'll round that down to twelve. Twelve times two and a half is thirty. Thirty times two and a half is seventy-five, and seventy-five times two and a half is 187.5.

Add all those numbers together, and the entire student body would be gone by next Monday. Sooner if the extra time available on the weekend allowed the students to be more active."

The Headmaster rubbed the bridge of his nose, warring with his instinctive reaction to yell. "Eight more students were caught trying to sneak down to the swamp this morning," he continued.

"Well, at that kind of exponential rate of increase, if you suspend everyone who tries to go see the yeti, you are going to be giving your entire teaching staff the day off by Friday."

"Yes, well, that can't happen, can it?" said the Headmaster.

Friday opened her mouth to answer, but the Headmaster interrupted.

"That was rhetorical."

Friday nodded.

"Something is going on," said the Headmaster. "I need to get to the bottom of it and stop it." He paused.

Friday clamped her lips together.

"But I am a sixty-seven-year-old man, and I do not want to go wandering about the swamp in the middle of the night," said the Headmaster. "And the only thing I want to do less than wander about the swamp is have another conversation with giggling schoolgirls."

"Then being a Headmaster seems like an odd career choice," said Friday.

The Headmaster just glared at her. He was about to ask for a favor, so he realized he shouldn't start yelling no matter how much he might dearly love to.

"You have apparently set yourself up as an in-house private detective," observed the Headmaster.

"The students here have a lot of problems," said Friday.

"Believe me, I know," agreed the Headmaster. "Now, I could conduct a systematic

investigation into this debacle: formally interview students, search their rooms, and post guards on the swamp. But I have found from experience that as soon as I start doing things like that, parents start sending lawyers to represent their children, I receive legal letters about search-and-seizure laws, and the gardeners' union demands triple pay for danger money. And then do you know what happens?"

Friday paused, then asked, "Is that a rhetorical question?"

"Yes it is—you're improving. Well done, Miss Barnes," said the Headmaster. "I'll tell you what happens. I learn nothing. I know nothing. Nothing is gained. If anything, I lose because the entire student body realizes that I am a toothless tiger they can ignore as they please."

"You seem very dissatisfied with your job," observed Friday. "Why don't you just retire?"

The Headmaster waved his hand as though literally waving the thought away. "Gambling debts," he said, as if those two words explained everything, as indeed they did. "So," continued the Headmaster, "that's where you come in."

"You want me to help you recoup your gambling debts, because you rightly guessed I'm capable of card counting?" asked Friday. She was finding it hard to follow the Headmaster's train of thought. He was obviously suffering some sort of existential crisis in parallel to the beast-in-the-swamp issue.

"No, I want you to investigate the swamp yeti," said the Headmaster. "Find out what is going on, and report back to me."

Friday considered this. Fortunately, she was very

clever, so she was able to run through a lot of variables and come up with a response in a short amount of time. "What's in it for me?" she asked.

The Headmaster considered this. Not many students would have the gall to ask such a blunt question. "You pay your own tuition, don't you?" said the Headmaster.

Friday nodded, realizing the Headmaster had been incredibly discreet if he had known this all along and yet no one else in the school did.

"If you find out what is going on so that this can all be settled respectably in the next twenty-four hours," said the Headmaster, "I will give you free tuition here for the first semester of next year."

Friday flinched. Tuition cost $14,000 per semester. The boarding fee was an additional $11,000 per semester. But still, if she agreed to the Headmaster's terms she could earn $14,000 in just one day, or rather one night because that was probably when everything would happen.

"Deal," said Friday, holding out her hand to the Headmaster. "I'll have the perpetrator in your office by dawn."

"If you do, I will be very cross," said the Headmaster. "I need my sleep. Make it eight o'clock."

Friday started to leave, then turned back. "I don't suppose it would be all right if I sat on your bench for the rest of the period? Mr. Blackmore insists on going on and on about the use of high-carbon steel in making hand tools, and it really is quite tedious."

"Go!" barked the Headmaster.

Wisely, Friday turned and left.

# 24

## The Plan

While the students in woodworking class were sanding their bookends, Friday took advantage of the bustle to quietly tell Melanie all about the Headmaster's proposal.

"Are you going to do it?" asked Melanie.

"Of course I'm going to do it," said Friday. "It's a wonderful mystery. I was going to get to the bottom of it anyway. But now that the Headmaster is paying me to investigate, then I've doubly got to. Because not only will I get lots and lots of

lovely money, but I'll also get let off if I'm caught doing anything I shouldn't in the process."

"Anything short of murdering someone," corrected Melanie. "I don't think even the Headmaster could let you off murder."

"That's all right—I doubt it will come to that," said Friday. "Although if it was self-defense, I'd get away with it. You always get away with murder if you make it look like self-defense."

"Yes," Melanie said. "But then you've got to incite someone into trying to murder you, and it strikes me that a lot could go wrong there."

"You're probably right," agreed Friday.

"Be quiet, girls," snapped Mr. Blackmore. "Concentrate on your sanding." Mr. Blackmore settled himself back into his chair so he could nod off again.

"So when do you start investigating?" whispered Melanie.

"Oh, I've already started," whispered Friday. "In my head." Friday tapped the side of her forehead as she said this. "I've started computing all the possibilities. But I shall actually, physically begin my investigation tonight after it gets dark, when I'll sneak down to the swamp and try to catch the beast myself."

"Gosh," said Melanie.

"I was hoping you would come with me," said Friday. "There will be a lot of equipment to carry, and if I do get abducted by a beast-man, I'll need you to rush back to the school and tell everyone about it."

"What if I get carried off by a beast-man?" asked Melanie.

"I won't allow that to happen," said Friday. "I'll bop him on the head with a stick if he tries."

"I thought you didn't know anything about violence or self-defense?" said Melanie.

"Oh, I don't now," admitted Friday, "but I've borrowed a book from the library on kendo. It won't take me long to read it, so I'll know all about the Japanese art of bopping people on the head with a stick by tonight."

"All right," said Melanie. "I'll do it."

"Girls!" snapped Mr. Blackmore. "You're ruining my nap!"

"Sorry, Mr. Blackmore," said Friday and Melanie in unison. Then they got back to their sanding. Friday looked about. She hadn't realized that Ian was standing so close behind her. But he didn't look like he was listening, except for the fact that his ears were pink.

When they went to bed that night Melanie instantly went to sleep. Nothing, not even an imminent confrontation with a wild and hairy creature of the night, could keep her from slipping into an unconscious REM state. It took all her powers of concentration to maintain a conscious non-REM state at the best of times.

Friday didn't sleep at all. She was too busy planning, triple-checking that the batteries in her flashlight were fully charged (which, ironically, was just running down the charge), and speed-reading her book on kendo. It turned out the martial art was way more complicated and involved a lot more yelling than she was comfortable with.

She and Melanie had decided to leave their excursion down to the swamp until 2:00 a.m. because that was when the other two groups of students had been attacked. Friday didn't see that there was anything to be gained by going to the swamp sooner, except perhaps hypothermia and an increased risk of leeches.

Friday's alarm rang at 1:50 a.m. exactly. Then she had to shake, gently slap, and finally tip a glass of water over Melanie to wake her up, too.

The girls snuck out of their room and down the stairs. Friday reflected that it really was silly for the school to cover its floors with such lovely carpet. It only made it much easier for all the students to sneak about quietly.

They were halfway across the lobby when their plan derailed. A light flashed right into their eyes.

"What's going on?" demanded Friday.

"I'm supposed to be asking that," said Miss Harrow.

"Oh, it's you," said Friday. "We were just sneaking down to the swamp to try to catch the beast."

"You and half the school," said Miss Harrow. "Well, it isn't going to happen. There will be a teacher on duty at this door and the back door all night. No one is sneaking anywhere, except right back to bed to get some sleep, which you need because I know for a fact you are doing a practical grid analysis of the insect life in the soccer field tomorrow."

"No, we're not," said Friday. "You didn't say anything in class."

"I just thought it up now," said Miss Harrow.

"That isn't very nice," said Melanie. "Usually you're very nice."

"Well, it's hard to be nice when you've been sitting in a hard-backed chair in the dark, waiting two hours for silly students to be silly."

"So just to confirm what we have discussed here," said Friday before the conversation got sidetracked any further, "you're not letting us out the front door and you are in an uncharacteristically bad mood, so we're unlikely to be able to change your mind."

"That is correct," said Miss Harrow.

"And there is another teacher on the back door?" asked Friday. "I don't suppose it's Mr. Blackmore?"

"No, it's Miss Brahms," said Miss Harrow, "and she has raging insomnia, so there is little chance she will be napping on the job."

"Oh dear," said Friday. "Then I suppose we had better return to our room and go back to sleep."

"You do that," said Miss Harrow.

The girls walked back to their room. "But what about the beast and the fourteen thousand dollars?" asked Melanie.

"I was lying," whispered Friday.

"We're not going back to our room?" asked Melanie.

"We're doing that," said Friday. "But we are not going back to sleep."

As soon as they got back in their room Friday rushed over to the window, threw up the sash, and looked out.

"You shut that window!" Mr. Blake, the economics teacher, called from outside.

"I was just getting some fresh air," called Friday.

"I don't believe you for a second," called Mr. Blake. "Now do as you're told."

Friday closed the window and drew the curtains.

"Couldn't you explain you're on orders from the Headmaster?" asked Melanie.

"Of course not," said Friday. "No one can know I have an authorized role. What if one of the teaching staff is the yeti?"

"I doubt it," said Melanie. "Teaching isn't a terribly glamorous or well-paid job. I think a beast-man could do better. Perhaps we should just go back to sleep."

Friday scowled. "Not on my watch." She opened her backpack and took out a pruning saw. It was a particularly vicious-looking hand tool about two feet long and with extremely sharp teeth.

"Are you going to cut Miss Harrow's legs off?" asked Melanie.

"How would that help us?" asked Friday.

"I don't know," conceded Melanie. "But sometimes I find it hard to predict what you're going to suggest next."

"I'm going to cut a hole in the ceiling," said Friday. "You push your desk over here, I'll balance my chair on top, and then I'll climb up and cut a hole big enough for us to climb through."

This process took quite a bit of time because neither of them was naturally athletic or coordinated. They would probably have been quicker if either of them had ever attended or participated in a PE class, but it was too late to start doing jumping jacks now.

After considerable effort, some swearing, and a lot of scraped fingers, the girls managed to haul themselves up into the roof cavity. It was not a pleasant place to be. The roof was sloping and full of crossbeams, so there were a lot of things to bang your head on. It also stank of mold and dead possums, probably because it was full of mold and dead possums, and a great deal of rat poo as well.

"I don't mean to sound critical," said Melanie, "but by climbing into the roof, aren't we moving in the opposite direction of where we need to be heading? I thought we were going down to the swamp."

"Yes, but we need to get out of the building first," said Friday. "And everyone expects students to escape by the doors or windows. No one expects them to climb into the roof, remove some roof tiles, and escape that way."

"Onto a slippery, sloping surface twenty feet off the ground?" asked Melanie. "I can see why they would think that is unlikely to happen."

Friday moved over to a higher part of the cavity,

where she could easily stand up and reach the roof above her. "I'll just cut through this insulation sheeting, then pop out some tiles, and we'll be away."

Unfortunately, cutting insulation is not tremendously easy. It makes a great deal of mess and dust, which leads to a tremendous amount of coughing. Eventually, Friday did manage to hack her way through to the ceramic roof tiles.

"Now how do you get them out?" asked Melanie.

"Well, roof tiles aren't attached to anything," said Friday. "There's no glue holding them together; they just slide into each other with matching grooves." This proved to be not quite correct. While there may be no glue, roof tiles are held in place by all the other roof tiles, neatly folded over each other and holding each other down with their weight. Unsurprisingly, Friday was unable to lift the weight of an entire roof's worth of tiles. It was now 2:10 and the girls really needed to get down to the swamp.

"We could always try the air vent," suggested Melanie.

"The what?" asked Friday.

"There is a rotating air vent over there," said

Melanie, pointing to a round heat extractor that vented hot air with its rotating sphere of blades.

"That would work," agreed Friday.

Fortunately, the air vent was much easier to disassemble than the tiles, and they were soon up on top of the roof.

"Now how do we get down?" asked Melanie.

"Have you ever tried rappelling?" asked Friday.

"No," said Melanie.

"Neither have I," admitted Friday. "But I looked it up on the Internet and it seems straightforward enough, so let's give it a go."

Friday took a coil of rope out of her backpack and looped one end around the brass weathercock that was welded on to the ridge pole. Then she took a rappelling harness out of her backpack.

"Do you want to go first?" she said, offering the harness to Melanie.

"No, it's all right," said Melanie. "You go and I'll watch."

Friday strapped herself in, clicked on the carabiner, and threw the rope over the side of the building.

"Wish me skill," said Friday.

"Don't you mean 'Wish me luck'?" asked Melanie.

"I'd much rather have skill than luck," said Friday. "Skill can be relied on. Luck can go bad."

With that she started walking backward down the roof, slowly feeding the rope out. When Friday got to the edge she looked over. The school's compost heap was directly below. Diego had just put a fresh batch of chicken poo on the pile, so it really stank. Friday correctly guessed that no teacher would be monitoring this area of the grounds with any great frequency. Taking a deep breath (and then immediately regretting it because it really did smell dreadful), Friday stepped out over the gutter and, holding herself perpendicular to the wall with the rope, began to walk backward toward the ground. Her confidence grew after a couple of steps, and she found the courage to take several large bounds backward and down. Then her confidence grew too much. She lost her grip on the rope and started plummeting the rest of the way, falling flat on her back on the compost heap.

Fortunately, if you don't have a pillow-top mattress handy, then a damp compost heap is an excellent thing to land on. Friday was totally unhurt.

"I'm okay," called Friday. "It's your turn."

"I know," Melanie called down, "but on reflection I've decided I don't want to do this."

"What?" said Friday.

"I think I'm going to climb back into the roof, then

back into our room, get back into bed, and go to sleep," said Melanie. "I think it would be more fun than risking falling off a roof, confronting a beast, and getting suspended from school. You're the best friend I've ever had, Friday. But I really, really don't want to get suspended—I would have to pack up all my things, and packing is exhausting."

Friday sighed. She would have argued with Melanie, but she could see that Melanie had a point. There was no logical argument Friday could use to persuade her, and Melanie was not the type of person to be swayed by logic anyway.

"All right," said Friday. "But if I do go missing, you must tell everyone what happened."

"That you fell in a stinky compost heap?" asked Melanie.

"No, that I went missing while looking for the beast of the swamp," said Friday.

"All right," said Melanie. "I'll write myself a little note before I go to bed so I won't forget."

Melanie's head disappeared over the side of the roof, and Friday was left alone in the darkness and the chicken poo.

Friday climbed out of the stinky brown pile of gunk;

scraped off the biggest, stinkiest pieces; and quietly crept to the edge of the building, where she carefully peered around. To the left there was no one. To the right, in the distance, she could see Miss Finnegan, the assistant librarian, but her back was turned.

Friday decided to risk it. She dashed across the yard to the cover of the bushes beyond. As soon as she started running, Friday realized she had made a terrible mistake. The distance between the building and the bushes was only about fifty yards. But Friday was not good at running. She had forgotten just how bad she was. She pumped her legs as fast as she could, but her body did not seem to be aerodynamic or coordinated. Running for her did not work in the same way it did for the athletes she had seen on television. And the backpack full of what she had thought were essential supplies was now a major encumbrance as it wobbled back and forth, making it even harder for her to retain her balance.

Friday glanced across at Miss Finnegan, who was starting to turn, but the bushes were still twenty yards away. Friday pushed forward, trying to run harder. But Miss Finnegan was sure to see her.

What Friday had not allowed for was Miss

Finnegan's motives. As she turned to dutifully continue her patrol, Miss Finnegan had indeed caught a flash of movement out of the corner of her eye. But Miss Finnegan was very tired from a long day of stamping books and arguing with students about library fines. She was also wearing a very nice pair of patent leather shoes, and on an assistant librarian's salary she could not afford an unlimited supply of patent leather shoes. So tiredness combined with the attractiveness of her footwear meant that the last thing Miss Finnegan wanted to do on her patrol of the school grounds was actually catch a student. She certainly didn't want to have to chase one into the swamp.

When she saw the movement in the corner

of her eye, she immediately stopped patrolling and bent down to tie her shoelace. She wasn't wearing shoes that had laces but she was very good at playing charades, so she took her time pretending to do double knots on both shoes and adjusting them for comfort. All of which meant that by the time she did stand up and look around, there was nothing to be seen because Friday had collapsed in a dense rhododendron bush, gasping for breath.

When Friday saw Miss Finnegan continue on her patrol and disappear around the far corner of the dormitory building, she got up and started making her way deeper into the swamp. There was a full moon, so she did not need the headlamp she had strapped to her scalp. She was easily able to make her way through the bogs and bushes, although not quite silently because she did occasionally fall down and have to yelp "Ow" or "Oomph," depending on how much she hurt herself.

She had been struggling forward into the ever boggier swamp for a full ten minutes when she heard a rustling in the bushes up ahead. Friday instinctively crouched down, then realized she would never catch the beast if she was crouching in a bush, so she stood up and started to creep forward. There was no sound ahead of her now. She stealthily made her way through the undergrowth, toward the place where she'd last heard movement.

Friday emerged into a clearing. It was about fifteen feet around and covered in grass, with wildflowers everywhere. Friday absentmindedly thought to herself, *What a lovely spot for a picnic,* when suddenly there was a crash and a loud rustle in the bushes and a beast leaped out in front of her, arms raised, gnashing his horrible pointed teeth and screaming, "Yaaagggghhhhh!"

Friday whipped her autographed baseball bat out of her backpack, held it high above her head, and did what the book on kendo had instructed. She screamed with terrifying vehemence, "Hiiiiiyaaaahhhh!!!"

As she lunged forward, the beast stumbled back

and Friday froze in her tracks. She peered through the inky gloom. "Ian Wainscott, is that you?"

The beast dropped his arms, pulled off his mask, and asked petulantly, "How could you tell?"

"Your costume," said Friday. "I can see a name tag sewn into the waistband."

Ian checked his hem and saw that Friday was correct. "My mother," grumbled Ian. "She sews name tags into everything."

"You're lucky," said Friday. "My mother can calculate the precise movement of the planets, but she can't sew, and even if she could, it would never occur to her to sew a name tag on for me."

"Thank you for the invitation to your own personal pity party," said Ian sarcastically. "I'd rather not attend."

"Nevertheless," said Friday, "you're coming with me to make a full confession to the Headmaster."

"I will not," said Ian.

"Fine, I'll report you, then," said Friday.

"You'd rat?" asked Ian. "Of course you would. Why would you care if you ruined my life?"

"You just tried to scare the living daylights out of me by jumping out and pretending you were a wild beast," objected Friday.

"There's always an excuse," muttered Ian.

"I'm going to go and wake up the Headmaster now," said Friday. "Unless you can give me a good reason why I shouldn't."

"Because I'm not the beast," sulked Ian.

"Really?" said Friday. "Because the head-to-toe hairy beast outfit does seem to contradict your statement."

"Well, yes, I'm dressed as a beast now," conceded Ian. "But it wasn't me the last two nights."

"Then why on earth have you dressed up like this tonight?" asked Friday.

"Because I overheard you talking to Melanie in woodwork," said Ian. "I knew you would be down here in the swamp after dark, and I wanted to scare you."

"Why?" asked Friday.

"None of your business," said Ian.

"Clearly it's my business," said Friday. "I'm the one you're trying to frighten."

"Well then, I'm not telling," said Ian.

"I never realized boys could be so complicated and hard to understand," said Friday, shaking her head. "I'm going to have to reread *Men Are from Mars, Women Are from Venus*."

Just then they heard a crash in the bushes, about a hundred yards away, then a lot of *shhh-shh-shhing* followed by a lot of giggling.

"What was that?" asked Ian.

"Let's find out," said Friday, and started making her way toward the new noise.

"Why should I?" asked Ian.

"What's the alternative?" asked Friday. "Go back to your dorm and fall asleep? Where's the fun in that?"

Friday kept making her way through the scrub, and soon Ian followed.

It was pretty easy to track them because whoever they were, they were making a lot of noise.

"That sounds like more than one beast," said Ian.

"I don't think it is a beast," said Friday. "From everything I've read about beasts, they don't giggle that much."

Friday and Ian pushed through a few more bushes, clambered over a mossy log, and then spotted them up ahead—seven girls sneaking through the swamp and giggling. When one of the girls suddenly screamed, Friday recognized Mirabella's voice.

"Aaaaaaghh!" said Mirabella.

"Shhhh, be quiet, you'll wake up the beast," shushed the other girls.

"I got some cobweb in my hair," complained Mirabella.

"Ew, gross," squealed the other girls before giggling some more.

"Come on, we've got to find that beast," said Mirabella.

"I hope he's cute," said another girl.

"Of course he's cute. When have you ever heard of a man who's been raised in the wild being unattractive?" said Mirabella.

More giggling.

"I hope he falls in love with me," said a third girl. "It would totally annoy my dad."

"I know," agreed Mirabella. "My dad practically would have an aneurysm if I had a boyfriend with an earring. So his head would totally explode if I went out with a wild ape-man who lived in a swamp."

The girls giggled some more.

Friday whispered to Ian. "I can't believe they are risking expulsion, not to mention spider bites and ankle injuries, just for the chance of meeting a handsome beast."

Ian shrugged. "Girls are stupid."

Friday turned and looked at Ian through the darkness. "You don't really mean that," she said. "You're just being provocative."

"You don't count as a girl," said Ian spitefully, "because you're so—"

At that moment Ian's insult was cut short by horrendous screaming.

The seven girls ahead of them clearly were not enjoying being scared, because there in front of them stood a hideous, terrifying, real monster. And unlike Ian in his pantomime attempt to scare Friday, this beast did not shriek or threaten to suck their blood. It bared its grizzled claws and hissed a low and menacing hiss. The girls screamed some more and then ran as fast as they could (which was a lot faster than Friday) back toward the school.

The beast pounded its fists on its chest and roared, then turned and disappeared into the depths of the swamp.

"Wow!" said Ian. "There really is a beast!"

*KABOOM!* came a loud crack of thunder.

Friday and Ian flinched.

"Of course there is," said Friday. "And now I know

exactly who it is. Come on, let's go back to the school so we can wake up the Headmaster."

Rain started to fall in great heavy drops.

"Okay," said Ian. He did not want to dally any longer in this suddenly ominous place.

Ian and Friday turned back toward the now wet path.

"Let's hurry," said Ian. "I don't like this." He rushed forward.

"Watch out for the tr—" Friday began.

But she couldn't get the words out before Ian tripped over a tree root.

"My ankle!" complained Ian.

"Is it sprained?" asked Friday.

"I don't know," said Ian. "I don't have a medical degree."

"There's no need to take that tone with me," said Friday.

"Oh, just shut up," said Ian.

And Friday did.

And so did Ian.

Because they were both grabbed from behind and had sacks roughly shoved over their heads.

# Chapter
# 25
# The Great Escape

Five minutes later, Friday and Ian were tied to chairs
and locked in a shed. At least they thought
they were. They couldn't be entirely
sure because they still had sacks
over their heads. But it felt like
they were tied to chairs. And
from the smell of fertilizer
and the echoey closeness of a
small room, they guessed that
they were locked inside
the groundskeeper's
storage shed down
by the edge of the

swamp. It was still raining, which was deafeningly loud on the tin roof.

"Great," said Ian. "How are we going to get out of this?"

"Just hold on a second," said Friday. "Give me a moment to consider our resources and I will come up with something."

Ian was silent for a full seventy-four seconds. "Come up with anything yet?" he asked.

"No," admitted Friday. "I can't believe I wasted all afternoon learning kendo. I should have been reading up on escapology. These ropes are really tight."

"They're not ropes—they're plastic zip ties," said Ian.

"Oh," said Friday.

"Police use them when they haven't got enough handcuffs to go around," said Ian.

"It must be three in the morning," said Friday. "In another five hours people will begin to notice that we're missing. And by nine they're sure to send out a search party. We'll just have to wait."

"I am not going to sit here zip-tied to a chair with a stinky sack over my head, listening to the most un-pleasant girl on the planet for six hours," said Ian.

"That's a bit harsh," complained Friday. "There are

a lot more unpleasant girls than me. Apart from the psychopaths and serial killers, there's Ursula in eighth grade, who is very rude."

"Shut up, I'm trying to concentrate," said Ian.

"Sorry," said Friday. Now it was her turn to fall silent.

Ian was quiet for a while. Then Friday could hear him rocking back and forth on his chair.

"What are you doing?" she asked.

"I've got an idea," said Ian. "Give me a sec."

There was silence for a second. Friday heard Ian grunt with strain as his chair creaked. There was the breeze of movement and suddenly a loud *smash* as she heard Ian land hard and the chair splinter beneath him.

A second later the sack was ripped off her head and she felt Ian's hand fumbling with her zip ties.

"What did you do?" asked Friday.

"A front flip," said Ian.

"But you were tied to a chair," said Friday.

"That's why the chair broke," said Ian, as he finally managed to cut off her zip ties with an old pair of pliers. "It was rickety to start with. Spinning 360 degrees and landing on it with my body weight was enough to finish it off."

"Wow, that's impressive," said Friday.

"I know," said Ian. "Come on, let's get out of here."

"All right," said Friday, walking over to the door. But when she tried the handle the door was locked.

"Stand aside," said Ian.

Friday took a step back.

Ian lifted his leg and delivered a kick that would have made a donkey proud, to the door just below the handle.

Then he collapsed on the floor, clutching his foot and writhing in pain.

"The door opens inward," said Friday. "To kick the door open, you'd have to kick the whole frame out."

"Why didn't you say so before I kicked it!" demanded Ian.

"I didn't expect you to kick it!" exclaimed Friday. "I thought that was obviously a stupid thing to do when there is a window over there we could easily smash through."

"Well, I'm not kicking that out," said Ian. "First, I sprained my ankle on a tree root. Now I've done goodness knows how much damage to ligaments in my knee because it didn't occur to you to mention that the door opened inward."

"And yet you managed to do a front flip, blindfolded and zip-tied to a chair," observed Friday. "You really are a strange and complicated boy."

Friday picked up the leg of the broken chair and used it to smash the windowpane out. Then she carried her unbroken chair over to the window, stepped up on it, and started to climb through.

"Hey!" cried Ian. "Aren't you going to help me?"

"In a second," said Friday as her bottom then her legs disappeared out the window, immediately followed by the sound of a thud as she hit the ground below.

"I can't follow you," protested Ian. "I've got injuries!" He tried struggling onto the chair. But he only toppled over onto a bag of poultry fertilizer (chicken poo), breaking the only previously unbroken chair.

Then there was a loud crunch and the door flew inward. Friday strode into the room. "You see?" she said. "That is how you kick open a door. What are you doing lying on the floor?"

"Just help me up," snapped Ian.

Friday pulled Ian to his feet. Then he put his arm heavily about her shoulder as she helped him limp to the doorway.

"This is just like a Tarzan movie," said Friday. "You're Jane with a sprained ankle—"

"Yes, I got the reference," said Ian through gritted teeth. He was clearly in a great deal of pain.

"At least you're not crying or screaming all the time," said Friday, trying to be nice, which was not a great strength of hers.

"Just shut up and let's get out of here as quickly as possible so we can get to the part where I never have to speak to you again," said Ian.

They hobbled out of the shed and into the drenching rain, where they were blinded by a bright light being shone straight into their faces.

"There they are!" declared Miss Harrow.

"You two have a lot of explaining to do," said the Headmaster.

# Chapter
## 26
# The Reckoning

Twenty minutes later, Friday and Ian, as well as Miss Harrow, Mirabella, her giggling friends, the Headmaster, and even Melanie (although she didn't really count because she kept drifting off to sleep), were gathered in the Headmaster's office. They all had towels draped around their shoulders. Even

the Headmaster looked significantly less dignified than usual, wearing a raincoat over his pajamas.

"What on earth have you been up to?" demanded the Headmaster as he glared accusingly at Friday.

"I don't know why you're cross with me," said Friday. "You asked me to investigate, and that's exactly what I did."

"I specifically said I did not want to have to go traipsing around the swamp in the middle of the night myself," said the Headmaster. "And look at this!" He held his foot in the air for Friday to examine. "My beautiful handmade Italian leather slippers are ruined!"

Friday leaned in and sniffed the shoe.

"Don't be disgusting!" denounced the Headmaster.

"They're not handmade Italian leather," said Friday. "They're a Chinese knockoff. You can tell because they're made of pig leather, not cow leather."

"Don't be ridiculous!" accused the Headmaster. "My wife gave me these for my birthday."

"Perhaps she was angry with you," said Friday. "Maybe about the gambling debts."

The Headmaster was turning red with anger.

"Go on," said Ian. "Keep talking. Then maybe he won't expel you; he'll murder you instead."

"What is going on?" demanded the Headmaster. "I was awoken by Miss Harrow to be informed that seven dripping-wet hysterical girls had turned up in the lobby, that there is a great big hole in the dormitory roof where someone had cut out a ventilator, causing rain-water to pour into Miss Van Der Porten's art class—"

"No great loss," said Friday. "She isn't a terribly good teacher. No instinctive grasp of light at all."

"And that two of my most troublesome students are missing in the swamp, presumed kidnapped by a swamp yeti," the Headmaster continued. "So, I repeat, what on earth is going on?!"

"A smuggler is using the school swamp to sneak contraband onto a boat headed overseas," said Friday.

"What?!" exploded the Headmaster. "I know full well that some or, rather, many members of our over-privileged student body get friends and employees to sneak electronic equipment into the school via the swamp. What has that got to do with beasts?"

"This smuggler is smuggling something far more serious," said Friday, "and using the beast to try to scare students away from the activities."

"He's trying to steal our hearts!" squealed Mira-bella.

All the other girls squealed like a hysterical Greek chorus.

The Headmaster sighed. "Girls, if you cannot calm yourselves down, I shall send you outside to stand in the rain so that the cold water will quell your hysteria. I will not have squealing in my office."

"The strategic error the smuggler made," said Friday, "was not allowing for the fact that a large percentage of teenage girls would dearly like to fall in love with a wild beast-man who wanders the swamp. So using this disguise actually made him a magnet for the more silly girls among the student body."

Mirabella sobbed as she realized she had been so accurately insulted.

"So are you the smuggler?" asked the Headmaster, turning to Ian. "You are the only person here dressed as a beast, and although it is not common knowledge, it is a fact that your family has financial problems."

"That's nobody's business," yelled Ian angrily as he leaped to his feet, then collapsed on the carpet because his ankle and knee hurt.

"Of course it isn't Ian," said Friday. "He has too much of a sense of honor."

"Does he?" said Melanie. "But he always does such dreadful things to you."

"Yes, but that's for an entirely different reason," said Friday.

"Ah yes," said Melanie, "because he's in love with you."

"No, I'm not!" exclaimed Ian.

"What was it Shakespeare said?" asked Melanie.

"He said a great deal of things," said Friday. "You'll have to be more specific."

"The lady doth protest too much," quoted Melanie.

Mirabella gasped. "Are you saying . . . that Ian is a lady?"

"No," said Friday. "She's saying he is in love with me because he says he isn't in love with me. Do try to keep up."

"I'm not in love with you!" exclaimed Ian.

"You see?" said Melanie, nodding and smiling knowingly.

"Miss Barnes," said the Headmaster as he rubbed his temples, trying to keep the inevitable migraine at bay, "could we please set aside discussions of your love life and concentrate on the matter at hand. Why is there a beast in my swamp?"

"Because Miss Harrow is a smuggler," said Friday.

Everyone turned and looked at Miss Harrow. She looked shocked. "This is preposterous."

"It was Melanie who put me on to it," said Friday.

"I did?" said Melanie. "I didn't realize I was so clever."

"Melanie notices things that other people don't," explained Friday. "She rarely notices anything she should. But occasionally she observes something apparently trivial that is in fact deeply intriguing. For example, one week ago she mentioned that she did not want to skip biology class because Miss Harrow always got new birds on Tuesdays."

"What is so intriguing about that?" asked the Headmaster.

"Have you ever paid close attention to Miss Harrow's bird collection?" asked Friday. "She has some remarkable specimens: a wide variety of parrots, native owls, and rare waterbirds."

"So? She's a biology teacher," said the Headmaster. "The aviary predates her. Miss Harrow has only been on staff for two years. The aviary has been here since the school was built eighty years ago."

"But parrots, owls, and even waterbirds are very

long-lived. Parrots can live up to fifty years. Why would new ones be appearing on Tuesdays unless old ones were going and, if so, going where? These birds are very expensive to buy. Even for a school like this. If half a dozen native birds were dropping dead every week and the school was paying thousands of dollars to replace them, then surely someone would notice."

"I haven't signed a check for new birds," said the Headmaster, turning to Miss Harrow.

"There are no new birds," said Miss Harrow. "Melanie is mistaken. You're not going to take her word for it, are you?"

"I wouldn't," admitted Melanie. "I'm not terribly reliable."

"You see?" said Miss Harrow.

"So if we went into your classroom and pulled up the loose sheet of linoleum that everyone always trips over as they enter," said Friday, "there wouldn't be a secret hidey-hole containing an old leather suitcase?"

"That suitcase is full of specimens from the swamp that I use in my lessons," asserted Miss Harrow.

"But what I'd like to know," said Friday, "is this: Does that suitcase have a secret bottom compartment that is currently full of cash?"

"This is absurd," said Miss Harrow. "How can you be saying these things? I've always gone out of my way to be kind to you."

"Which is, in itself, suspicious," said Friday, "because I am not a terribly nice or easy-to-get-along-with person."

"Here, here," said Ian.

"I like Friday," said Melanie. "She always tells me the answers to the math homework because she says it is a waste of my brain space for me to learn algebra."

"Really?" said the Headmaster.

"This is all ridiculous, unprovable speculation," said Miss Harrow. "I'll be talking to my lawyer."

"Not you, too," said the Headmaster. "It's bad enough with all the students consulting their lawyers every time a staff member holds a pop quiz."

"Actually, I can prove it all," said Friday. She got up and walked over to the window, pulled aside the curtain, and knocked on the windowpane.

"She has gone insane," said Ian. "Probably delirious from having a fertilizer bag over her head and inhaling all that nitrogen."

Out in the cold dark night a hand reached up and knocked on the far side of the pane.

The girls shrieked.

The Headmaster winced.

Friday threw open the window. And the hand, now joined by another hand, pushed Miss Harrow's old leather suitcase up and into the room. Friday leaned out the window. "Thanks, Binky, good work."

"Happy to help," Binky said merrily from outside in the rain.

Friday closed the window again.

"When I planned my excursion into the swamp tonight," said Friday, "I took the precaution of asking Binky to keep watch on whoever emerged from the swamp first, to follow them, and if they hid any large piece of luggage or storage container, to wait until they were gone, then steal it and bring it here. Or, rather, wait outside the window of the Headmaster's office."

"He carried it out perfectly," said Melanie proudly.

"Yes," said Friday. "The one thing Binky excels at is following instructions without thinking."

"He gets that from our father," said Melanie. "All the Pelly men are good at not thinking."

"Shall we see what's inside the suitcase?" asked Friday.

"No," said Miss Harrow. "This is an illegal search. You've got no business searching my property."

"But this is school property," said Friday. "See here." Friday pointed to a label by the handle that clearly read *Property of Highcrest Academy*. "And Binky found this in a school classroom, so there can be absolutely no problem with us taking a little look."

Friday clicked open the metal latches and lifted the lid of the case. The case was full of empty toilet paper rolls. Dozens of them.

"Toilet paper rolls!" exclaimed the Headmaster. "If Miss Harrow has been smuggling toilet paper out of the school, I should be slightly disappointed, but I would say that is more of a surprising misdemeanor than a serious transgression."

Friday picked up a toilet paper roll and looked at it closely. Then she sniffed it.

"Must you sniff everything?" asked the Headmaster. "You are supposed to be learning ladylike manners at this school."

"Toilet paper rolls are used by bird smugglers," said Friday. "They anesthetize the birds, then slide them into a toilet paper roll as packaging. So if the birds wake up, they can't open their wings and harm themselves."

"Toilet paper rolls are also used to hold toilet paper," observed Miss Harrow.

"There is no cash in the suitcase," said Friday, inspecting it closely, "and there are no secret compartments."

"No," said Miss Harrow. "No proof for your wild and defamatory accusations at all."

"So if they are not paying you in cash," said Friday, "what are they paying you in?"

Friday looked at the refuse she had emptied from the suitcase onto the desk. She rifled through it. There were dozens of toilet paper rolls, petri dishes, microscope slides, and a jam jar full of dirt. Friday picked up the jam jar and peered inside. Then she opened the lid and tipped the dirt all over the floor.

"My carpet!" exclaimed the Headmaster. "That will never come out. Manuela will kill me!"

Friday knelt down and sifted through the dirt.

"The particles are going into the fibers!" exclaimed the Headmaster.

And they were. The smaller pieces of dirt were falling between the carpet fibers, leaving the larger clumps of dirt and rock sitting on top. Friday tapped them with a pencil, spreading them all out. As she did this the others began to notice that some of the rocks were shiny. Very shiny.

"What is that?" asked Ian.

Friday held one of the clear shiny rocks up to her eye. The light from overhead hit it and refracted into sparkles. "Diamonds," said Friday.

Miss Harrow leaped up and tried to bolt. She ran first to the door, but it was locked. The Headmaster always locked his office door when he had meetings with hysterical girls so that their lawyers couldn't burst in unexpectedly.

"You'll never catch me!" cried Miss Harrow, which was entirely true because no one in the room tried. No one in the group was in the least athletically inclined except Ian, and he was injured. Miss Harrow ran over to the window, threw up the sash, and leaped out into the rain-soaked night. Unfortunately, she had not realized that Binky was still standing there. How could she? Anyone with common sense would have assumed that he would go and find somewhere dry to wait once he had served his purpose. But that was not Binky's way. No one had told him to go somewhere warm and dry, so he stayed cold and wet beneath the windowsill until his favorite biology teacher suddenly and unexpectedly jumped out and landed on his head.

"Ooomph," said Miss Harrow as her head clunked into Binky's.

"Are you all right, Miss?" asked Binky politely.

But his head was hard, and Miss Harrow was no longer conscious.

"You'd better carry her back inside, boy," called the Headmaster, leaning out the window.

"I'll help," said an authoritative voice from the bushes.

"Am I hearing things?" asked Melanie. "Or did that bush just offer to help?"

"It is I, Diego," declared the voice from the bushes as he stepped forward and revealed himself to be Diego the gardener. "I have been secretly watching Miss Harrow for months."

"Of course," agreed Melanie, "because you are in love with her."

"No," said Diego, "because I am a police officer with the elite countersmuggling unit."

"As am I," declared another voice from yet another bush. She stepped out and revealed herself to be Manuela, the cleaner.

"Manuela," gasped the Headmaster. "How could you deceive me? You're the best cleaner I've ever had."

"I told you her skill set was too advanced for her pay grade," said Friday, nodding her head wisely.

Manuela and Diego then helped Binky carry Miss Harrow, who was unconscious and handcuffed, back into the Headmaster's office, where they could continue their discussion in less rain-drenched conditions.

"We were sent here to survey the school because we believed rare birds were being smuggled out through the swamp," explained Manuela.

"But why would anyone pay large amounts of money for a bunch of birds?" asked the Headmaster. "They all just look brown and fluffy to me."

"In South America there are some wealthy and competitive bird collectors who love to outdo each other with the rarity of their specimens," explained Manuela.

"And in Korea," said Diego, "hearing the song of the lesser spotted woodpecker is believed to help with exam preparation."

"Urrrgh," groaned Miss Harrow. She was starting to come around.

The Headmaster went over and sat next to her.

"Miss Harrow," he said, "why would you do this? You are a beloved and cherished member of the Highcrest staff. You're actually good at teaching, which is more than I can say for ninety percent of the teachers here. Please say you have some sort of mitigating psychological condition so that I won't have to fire you."

"I did it for the money," said Miss Harrow. "I wanted to make enough to start a new life. I don't mind teaching. It's being around children that I can't stand."

"I knew it!" said Friday. "No one likes working with children."

"You'll have to fire her, sir," said Diego. "She's going to get five to ten years in a federal prison. Smuggling is a serious crime."

"Plus think of the poor birds," added Melanie.

And so Miss Harrow was led away. The school lost the best biology teacher, the best cleaner, and the best gardener it had ever had.

## Chapter

# 27

## In Conclusion

"Things have turned out rather well, in my opinion," said Friday.

It was Tuesday afternoon and she and Melanie were sitting in the dining room eating chocolate cake, after finishing second helpings of Mrs. Marigold's shepherd's pie.

Binky had been made a prefect for his outstanding effort at standing where he had been told to.

Melanie had been diagnosed with attention surfeit disorder, which

meant she did not have to take any more exams for the rest of the academic year because her psychologist decided that she would find them too confronting.

And Friday's fees were all paid up in advance for the next semester, which meant, mercifully, that she would not have to stay at home and go to public school.

"Everything has ended happily ever after," declared Friday, who was not normally a romantic, but she was feeling particularly buoyant, no doubt due to the high level of carbohydrates in the chocolate cake.

"Except for you and Ian," said Melanie.

"What about me and Ian?" asked Friday.

"You still haven't admitted that you love each other," said Melanie.

"We don't love each other," said Friday.

"You see?" said Melanie, as if Friday had proved her point.

"Ian hates me with a passion," said Friday.

"But why on earth would he hate you?" asked Melanie. "True, your cardigans are unpleasant and your green porkpie hat is eccentric, but he could just avert his eyes."

"He hates me," said Friday, "because he is the scholarship student."

"He is?!" exclaimed Melanie. "But that doesn't make any sense. If he is the scholarship student, he should like you for drawing all the attention away from him."

"He hates me," explained Friday, "because I made him the scholarship student. Wainscott is his mother's maiden name. His father's name is Friedricks. And he is the man I put in prison for insurance fraud, winning the reward that allowed me to pay my tuition."

"Oooh," said Melanie as she tried to process all this information, then gave up. "But how did you know?"

"Because he hates me so much," said Friday. "I've never had that effect on anyone. And I was really annoying to my elementary school teachers. It was the chair flip that decided it. It was so athletic. No twelve-year-old could do that unless he had advanced circus training, and what twelve-year-old might have had advanced circus training? A boy whose father majored in acrobatics at the Barnum and Bailey Circus Skills University. Then you add into that the mysterious, poorly prepared presentation on Egypt and his absence from school for a week. I called my uncle and found out that one Ian Friedricks Wainscott was a witness at his own father's trial that week."

"Ahhh," said Melanie. "Then he must really be in love with you."

"What?" said Friday, baffled.

"If he just hated you," said Melanie, "he'd have pushed you down a flight of stairs. But to implode your pencil box, stick your clothes on top of a channel marker, and follow you into the swamp dressed as a beast? That takes real devotion, attention to detail, and obsessive thinking. It's true love, just like in the movies."

"Barnes," snapped a voice behind them.

Friday and Melanie turned around.

The Headmaster was standing next to a uniformed police officer.

"What's this?" asked Friday. "Am I getting some sort of citizenship citation for everything I've done for the school?"

"No," said the Headmaster soberly, "I'm afraid not."

"Friday Barnes," said the police officer, "I'll have to ask you to come with me."

"Why?" asked Friday, as a feeling of dread sank down into her stomach.

"Because I'm arresting you," said the police officer.

*To be continued . . .*

# GOFISH

## R. A. SPRATT

**What did you want to be when you grew up?**
An intrepid world traveler.

**When did you realize you wanted to be a writer?**
When a TV producer said "We'd like to offer you a job as a writer."

**What's your most embarrassing childhood memory?**
Why would I tell you that?

**What's your favorite childhood memory?**
When I was eight my mum (or *mom* as you say in America) took me to England to visit our family there. The town my English family comes from is called Dursley (it's where J. K. Rowling got the name for the Dursleys in Harry Potter), and the post office sold candy. It was all candy that was entirely different from what we had in Australia. The feeling of walking into that store for the first time must have been what Christopher Columbus felt like sighting the Americas for the first time—that a wondrous, exciting journey of discovery had just begun. They had candy in giant jars and you could pick out what you wanted. The shopkeeper would then measure it out on an old-fashioned set of scales. It was all so wonderful.

**As a young person, who did you look up to most?**
I'm Australian. We don't look up to people. We don't want to give them swollen heads.

**What was your favorite thing about school?**
I had a really nice biology teacher who let me take my shoes off in class.

**What were your hobbies as a kid? What are your hobbies now?**
I rang church bells. I know it's a weird hobby, but everyone in my family has been doing it for over a hundred years.

   Now I still ring church bells, but my main hobby is CrossFit. I love working out with my friends.

**Did you play sports as a kid?**
No. Although my mother always said that if worrying was an Olympic sport, then I could represent Australia and win the gold medal.

**What was your first job, and what was your "worst" job?**
My first proper job was when I left home at 18 and went to work for a pharmaceutical services company (they managed the data on drug trials) as a technical assistant (dogsbody).

   I've had a lot of truly awful jobs because I've worked in TV for twenty years. The worst ones are when the top boss forces the middle boss to hire you then the middle boss spends every waking moment trying to make you quit. Those jobs tend to involve a lot of crying.

**What book is on your nightstand now?**
Hah! My night stand is like a Jenga game of books. Occasionally the stack gets too high and they avalanche onto my

laundry basket. There are at least two dozen stacked on there. Plus my Kindle with another couple dozen I've got on the go. They include a lot of regency romance novels, *A Game of Thrones*, the most recent in the No. 1 Ladies' Detective Agency series, *The Candymakers* by Wendy Mass, and lots of Agatha Christie books—I just finished *Murder on the Orient Express* and started *Death on the Nile*.

**How did you celebrate publishing your first book?**
I got my first book contract when I was in the hospital maternity ward the day after giving birth to my first child, so I had other things on my mind.

**Where do you write your books?**
In my home office. I've got a very nice office. It's very messy. But I like that.

**What challenges do you face in the writing process, and how do you overcome them?**
The Internet is very distracting. And I am very passionate about napping. But I find if I eat enough chocolate I can stay focused long enough each day to have a book at the end of six months.

**What is your favorite word?**
*Awesome*. For two reasons: (1.) I like to be very positive. (2.) I enjoy that it irritates people. I realize that these two reasons are, in a way, contradictory.

**If you could live in any fictional world, what would it be?**
I really like my real world. I have an excellent life. I love Jane Austen but I would not want to live in a world with eighteenth-century plumbing.

**Who is your favorite fictional character?**
I don't really have just one. I really like Scarlett O'Hara from *Gone with the Wind*. Deeply unpleasant people are oft maligned in literature. And yet in real life, ruthless, driven people are the people who get things done. I always think of her when critics equate a character's flaws with a book's flaws.

**What was your favorite book when you were a kid? Do you have a favorite book now?**
I love the Garfield cartoons, Asterix comics, and *Hating Alison Ashley* by Robin Klein. *Persuasion* by Jane Austen is probably my all-time favorite novel.

**If you could travel in time, where would you go and what would you do?**
I think it takes a level of dissatisfaction with your current life that I do not have to think about these things.

I think it would be irresponsible to try and change history. And I think it would be unimaginably unpleasant to live in an earlier age when plumbing was substandard and infectious diseases were rife.

**What's the best advice you have ever received about writing?**
Read your work aloud during the editing process.

**What advice do you wish someone had given you when you were younger?**
Spelling, high school English, and storytelling are three different things. Just because you're bad at the first two doesn't mean you will be bad at the third. And the third is a tricky bit—it's like weaving a magic spell.

**Do you ever get writer's block? What do you do to get back on track?**
Not really. Writer's block is something you get when you can't think of anything good to write. I've spent the last twenty years swamped with deadlines. When I can't think of anything good to write I just write the best I can. But it's amazing how often, when you go back, you realize your best that day was better than you realized. You have to have faith in your own ability to practice your craft.

**What do you want readers to remember about your books?**
Laughing. Thinking new ideas.

**What would you do if you ever stopped writing?**
Become a high school science teacher.

**Do you have any strange or funny habits? Did you when you were a kid?**
Everything I do is perfectly normal. The things the rest of you do—that's weird.

**What do you consider to be your greatest accomplishment?**
Getting married. I am a very odd person. It seriously shocked a lot of people that I found someone who would want to marry me.

**What would your readers be most surprised to learn about you?**
In the eighties, I worked as a supermodel in Milan. (I didn't, but it would surprise my readers to learn that.)

**W**ill Friday be arrested and thrown in prison?

**W**ill she and Melanie finish their
chocolate cake first?

**A**nd will Friday ever admit she is
madly in love with Ian Wainscott?

To find out what happens, read the second
book in this series. . . .

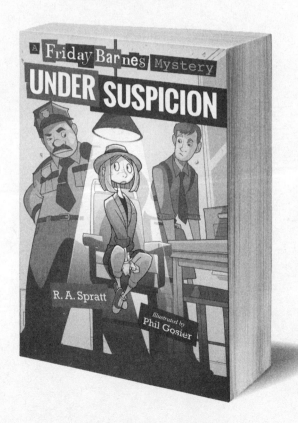

Turn the page for a sneak peek!

Friday Barnes and her roommate, Melanie Pelly, were sitting in the dining hall at Highcrest Academy, enjoying second helpings of chocolate cake. For two people who had absolutely nothing in common, except their mutual dislike of all sports, Friday and Melanie could not be better friends. They were more than just BFFs; they had formed a symbiotic relationship. Melanie was very vague, so she relied on Friday for basic information like what day of the week it was, what class they were sitting in, and how to do quadratic equations. Whereas Friday was socially clueless, so she relied on Melanie for intuitive knowledge, like telling her when she was being so irritating that her teacher was about to have a brain aneurysm.

Friday had never expected to attend a fancy private boarding school. That was until she received a $50,000 reward for helping her uncle solve a bank robbery. Coming from a highly academic family (both her parents and all four of her siblings had PhDs in physics), Friday decided to invest the money in her education, which was how she came to be at Highcrest.

Since arriving at the elite preparatory school, Friday had gone from being a scruffy eleven-year-old social outcast to being a brilliant eleven-year-old private detective. She'd had to because Friday didn't come from a wealthy family like the other students, so working as a private detective was her way of earning an allowance. Friday was still scruffy and socially outcast, but people were prepared to overlook that when they desperately needed her help.

And Friday didn't just help her fellow students. Even the Headmaster called on Friday when he had a problem he couldn't, or didn't want to, handle himself.

On this particular occasion, Friday and Melanie were at the end of a long week of searching for a swamp yeti, capturing bird smugglers, and saving the school's reputation, so Mrs. Marigold, the cook, felt they had earned an extra serving of dessert. But their calorie-induced bliss was about to be interrupted.

"Barnes," snapped a voice from behind them.

Friday and Melanie turned around. The Headmaster was standing next to a uniformed police sergeant.

"What's this?" asked Friday. "Am I getting some sort of citizenship award for everything I've done for the school?"

"No," said the Headmaster soberly. "I'm afraid not."

"Friday Barnes," said the police sergeant, "I have to ask you to come with me."

"Why?" asked Friday.

"Because I'm arresting you," said the police sergeant. "You are not obliged to say anything unless you wish to do so, but whatever you say or do may be used in evidence. Do you understand?"

"Not really," said Friday. "Not the situation anyway. But I do have a large vocabulary and as such have no trouble understanding the meaning of your words."

The police sergeant had dealt with people much more intimidating than Friday resisting arrest, so he simply took the matter in hand. He pulled Friday's chair back for her while she was still sitting on it, took her by the elbow, and guided her to her feet.

Friday was mortified. She didn't have to look up to know that everyone in the room was staring at her. This would be yet another reason for all her rich class-mates to snigger and laugh at her. There was nothing she could do. She was the most exciting spectacle in the dining room since Mrs. Marigold lost her temper with a vegetarian student-teacher and dumped a pud-ding on his head.

"If you'll come with me," said the police sergeant,

although Friday could barely hear him through the rushing sound in her ears. People always marvel that holding a seashell to your ear replicates the sound of the sea, but in the seconds before you faint the movement of blood rushing out of your brain replicates the sound of the sea, too.

Friday saw Melanie's concerned expression, and then something made her look across the room. Ian Wainscott, the most handsome boy in school (also the most infuriatingly smug boy in school), was entering through the back door. He was Friday's nemesis/love interest, no one was entirely sure which. In the past, she'd put his father in prison for a case of insurance fraud

involving a stolen diamond, and Ian had dressed up as a swamp yeti and tried to scare her to death. Yet they seemed to be magnetically drawn to each other, if for no other reason than to bicker.

Friday watched Ian's face as he took in the scene. He seemed surprised for a moment; then he caught Friday's eye, and his face returned to its normal apathetic mask.

The police sergeant started pulling at Friday's arm and the world seemed to return to normal speed. Her ears started to process sound again, just in time to hear the first murmurs of malicious gossip.

It was at times like this when Friday wished she didn't have a brain like a supercomputer. Having a photographic memory meant that the words, and the associated hurt, would be accessible in the long-term storage of her brain's neural matrix forever.

"Typical scholarship kid, probably been stealing," whispered Mirabella Peterson.

"Maybe she's being arrested for wearing those brown cardigans," said Trea Babcock. "She should get five to ten years for crimes against fashion."

"Plus another ten for the green hat," said Judith Wilton.

Now dozens of people sniggered. That was the last

Friday heard as the dining room door flapped closed behind her.

A squad car with lights flashing was parked at the top of the school's driveway.

"The Headmaster is going to hate that," said Friday. "It's a bad look for the school."

"The Headmaster will be grateful I'm taking you off his hands after what y— Wagh!" said the police sergeant, who was interrupted midlecture because he had fallen into a hole about one foot round and one foot deep. "Ow, that hurt," he said, rubbing his knees.

"I wonder who put that there?" said Friday. She inspected the hole. It looked like it had been dug out by hand.

"This crazy school," muttered the police sergeant. "There's always something going on. Rich kids with their weird pranks or bitter teachers with their revenge plots. The sooner we get out of here, the better."

Friday looked back at the main building. She had a lump in her throat and her eyes started to itch. She knew she wasn't suffering from pollen allergies because it wouldn't be spring for another six months.

Friday wasn't terribly in touch with her emotions, but she was able to deduce that she was upset. Being forced from Highcrest Academy was affecting her more than she would have imagined. The police sergeant was entirely right. Highcrest Academy was full of obnoxious children and strange teachers, but it had also become her home. She had friends—well, one friend. And she received three warm meals a day. So despite the Gothic architecture and the even more Gothic attitudes of the staff, this place had made her feel safe and needed—in a way her family home never had. As the squad car started to pull down the driveway, Friday hoped this would not be the last time she saw her school.

The police car wound its way through the rolling countryside to the nearest town. A female police officer was driving. They were heading for Twittingsworth, a fashionable and well-to-do rural area where the weekend homes of city bankers and lawyers were nestled among local farms.

"So what crime am I being accused of committing?" asked Friday.

"We'll discuss all that in the formal interview," said the police sergeant.

"Why, is it some sort of surprise?" asked Friday.

"It's a very serious offense," said the police sergeant.

"We don't want to jeopardize the case by deviating from correct procedure. We're going to do this by the book. There will be a lot of scrutiny. The National Counterterrorism Center has been alerted."

"Counterterrorism!" exclaimed Friday. "But I haven't done anything."

The police sergeant snorted. "Save it for the interview."

The police station was an old stone building, built back in the day when people had taken pride in the appearance of official institutions.

Friday had not been handcuffed. No doubt there were rules about handcuffing children. She also thought it unlikely that her own thin, spindly wrists could be contained by the same handcuffs that would be needed to restrain a fully grown man.

It was the policewoman who led Friday into the building, taking her through to an open-plan area where there were half a dozen desks cluttered with mountains of paperwork. There was one separate office partitioned off at the end of the room, no doubt for the sergeant. There were two doorways on the side. They looked like they led to cells, but they were marked "Interview

Room 1" and "Interview Room 2." A wooden bench sat between them.

Everything inside the police station was gray-green except for the cheerful posters on the wall, featuring famous athletes urging citizens to be respectful of women's rights.

Friday was underwhelmed. She had imagined the inside of a police station to be a more exciting place, but she supposed they could not put up gruesome crime-scene photos on the wall. As a result the police station looked like an average boring office.

Friday sat down on a wooden bench outside the interview rooms. The bench reminded Friday of the one outside the Headmaster's office, although on the whole it was more comfortable. Plus, the police station had less of a feel of impending doom than the Headmaster's office.

On the far end of the bench sat a man who looked like a vagrant, though a strangely large and athletic vagrant. He had been handcuffed to the seat. It was hard to gauge his height because he was sitting down, but he must have been well over six feet tall. He had thinning blond hair and a rough beard. His clothes were old, worn, and crumpled. And Friday noticed that he smelled quite distinctly of mold, even though she was trying her very best not to breathe through her nose. Friday felt like she had been put next to the lion enclosure at the zoo.

The policewoman bent down to speak to Friday in what she clearly hoped was a comforting fashion. "We've left a message for your mom and dad," she said, "so they should be here soon."

"I doubt it," said Friday. "They never check their messages. They only have an answering machine because they find it less irritating than letting their phone ring."

"How do you get in touch with them, then?" asked the policewoman.

"I don't," said Friday. "I suppose I could send an e-mail to one of my mother's PhD students and ask them to speak to her in person. That's what I did the time I broke my ankle on a geology excursion."

"You did?" asked the policewoman.

"Yes," said Friday. "I needed to let Mom know I wouldn't be home because the rescue helicopter couldn't pick me up from the cliff face until daylight. But I haven't done that for ages, because we're not allowed to have e-mail access at Highcrest Academy.

They have a strict anti-technology policy. They're frightened that students will use handheld electronic devices against the staff."

"Really?" said the policewoman.

"Yes," said Friday. "But students find ways around it. I know a girl who only took art so she could sketch incriminating drawings of her history teacher and mail them to her lawyer."

"This is a problem," said the policewoman. "We can't interview you until a family member is present."

"By 'interview' you mean browbeat me into confessing, don't you?" asked Friday.

"Well, um . . ." began the policewoman.

"It's all right," Friday assured her. "As a fledgling detective, I'd enjoy seeing professionals at work. Will you do 'good cop, bad cop,' or are you doing it already and that's why you're being nice to me?"

"Well, er—" said the policewoman, blushing a little at having been caught out by an eleven-year-old.

"This is exciting," interrupted Friday. "Call my Uncle Bernie. He's an insurance investigator. I'll write his number down for you. He'll come right away. I can't wait to get started."

Friday knew it would take some time for her uncle to get to the police station. His office was two hours away, and if he was cross-examining a hostile insurance claimant he might not be able to leave work immediately. So Friday reasoned that she had between two and a half and four hours to fill.

She took out a lollipop and stuck it in her mouth,

then looked around the room. She thought of asking for a crossword puzzle, but since she was very good at those it would probably only fill up five or six minutes.

Friday considered asking if she could read the police files, but she suspected there'd be some privacy law preventing the officers from showing them to a child. Also, it'd probably rub the police the wrong way if she read through their files and solved all their cold cases for them.

Friday glanced at the vagrant at the far end of the bench. He didn't look like the chatty type. He looked more the "hit you over the head with a rusty iron bar" type. Friday decided to leave him alone. She pulled a paperback from her pocket and started to read. She'd only been reading for a few minutes when she realized the vagrant was watching her. He hadn't turned and stared, but he was definitely watching her out of the corner of his eye. Friday looked up at him.

"Good book?" asked the vagrant.

Friday hadn't expected the vagrant to engage her in a literary discussion.

"It is, actually," said Friday. "It's E. M. Dowell's *The Curse of the Pirate King*, the story of a privileged boy who defies his family's expectations and runs away to be a pirate, then becomes enormously successful sailing the high seas and winning sword fights with people who are even more dubious than himself. We have to read it for English."

"They let you read that at school?" he asked. "In my day it was all Shakespeare and Dickens."

"The school is particularly proud of this book because it was written by the great-great-grandson of the school's founder, Sebastian Dowell," explained Friday. "E. M. Dowell is one of the few ex-students to become rich and famous without violating insider trading laws."

"Okay," said the vagrant. He didn't have an expressive face, but he seemed bemused.

"It's very exciting. We're all dying to know how it ends," continued Friday. "There's one more book to go in the series. Legend has it that E. M. Dowell came up with the idea for the whole series while he was at our school and that he wrote the last chapter first, then hid it. Like it was pirate treasure."

"Sounds like a weirdo," said the vagrant.

"Yes," agreed Friday. "Although the literary biographies phrase it differently. Their euphemism is 'eccentric recluse.'"

The vagrant snorted a laugh and went back to staring into the middle distance.

Now that she knew he wasn't terrifyingly dangerous, Friday was curious. "What have they busted you for?" she asked.

"What's it to you?" asked the vagrant.

"I'm up on terrorism charges," said Friday.

The vagrant raised an eyebrow.

"I didn't do it," said Friday. "I'm wrongly accused."

The vagrant snorted again.

"Look, I know I look like a child, mainly because I *am* only eleven years old," said Friday, "but I am actually a successful private investigator. I've solved a bank robbery and thwarted a bird-smuggling ring, as well as lots of smaller cases. Why don't you tell me your story? Perhaps I can help."

The vagrant didn't look at Friday, but he didn't look away either. He was clearly thinking about it.

"I'm waiting for my uncle to get here so I can be interviewed," volunteered Friday. "What are *you* waiting for?"

"Their computer to identify my fingerprints," said the vagrant.

"So you're refusing to tell them who you are?" asked Friday.

The vagrant shrugged. "I didn't do anything wrong, so why should I help them?"

"Interesting tactic," said Friday, admiringly. "But aren't you worried that you'll make them angry by being unnecessarily uncooperative?"

"Cops are always angry whatever you do," said the vagrant. "They have an awful job dealing with horrible people all day long. Time-wasting is the least of their worries. In fact, they quite like it because it increases their chances of getting overtime."

"All right, then," said Friday. "Since we're both stuck here for the next couple of hours, give me something to do. Tell me the details of your case."

The vagrant sighed. He was obviously weighing his options. He seemed to be the type of man who preferred to remain silent when possible.

"They say I stole a blue sapphire bracelet," said the vagrant.

"Did you?" asked Friday.

"No," said the vagrant.

"So why do they think you did?" she asked.

The vagrant shrugged. Then he looked down at his clothes. "Look at me, I'm a bum."

Friday nodded. She sucked her lollipop as she thought about it. Truth be told, she wasn't dressed much better herself. But it is a fact of life that some people can wear un-ironed earth tones and look like eccentric academics, and some people look like hobos who have been sleeping under a bush for a week.

"Take me through the details," urged Friday.